PRAISE FOR NANCY YOUNG MOSNY'S

Pieces of Gold

"*Pieces of Gold* is wonderfully
successful. . . . [A] skillfully crafted
first novel . . . keenly observant."

—JOHN ESPEY, author of
*Minor Heresies, Major Departures:
A China Mission Boyhood*

"Wonderful . . . Nancy's fluid writing and dry
wit reveal the dual nature of every parent
and child relationship."

—FAY CHEW MATSUDA,
Executive Director,
Museum of Chinese in the Americas

"Heartwarming . . . Nancy Young Mosny's book,
Pieces of Gold, is indeed a treasure."

—ELAINE L. CHAO,
Distinguished Fellow
at The Heritage Foundation

NANCY YOUNG

MOSNY

Bantam Books

NEW YORK LONDON TORONTO

SYDNEY AUCKLAND

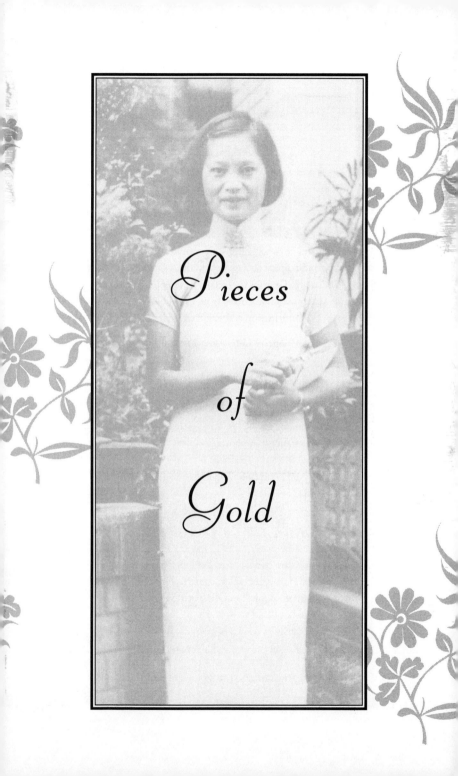

Pieces

of

Gold

MAY - 3 1999

PIECES OF GOLD

A Bantam Book / March 1999

All rights reserved.
Copyright © 1999 by Nancy Young Mosny.
Cover art and design copyright © 1999 by Honi Werner.

BOOK DESIGN BY DANA LEIGH TREGLIA

No part of this book may be reproduced or transmitted
in any form or by any means, electronic or mechanical,
including photocopying, recording, or by any
information storage and retrieval system, without
permission in writing from the publisher.
For information address: Bantam Books.

Library of Congress Cataloging-in-Publication Data
Mosny, Nancy Young.
Pieces of gold / Nancy Young Mosny.
p.   cm.
ISBN 0-553-38020-6
I. Chinese Americans—New York (State)—New York—
Fiction.   2. Chinese Americans—New Jersey—Fiction.
I. Title.
PS3563.0884565T48   1999
813'.54—dc21   98-39512
CIP

Published simultaneously in the United States and Canada

Bantam Books are published by Bantam Books, a division
of Random House, Inc. Its trademark, consisting of the
words "Bantam Books" and the portrayal of a rooster,
is Registered in U.S. Patent and Trademark Office and
in other countries. Marca Registrada. Bantam Books,
1540 Broadway, New York, New York 10036.

PRINTED IN THE UNITED STATES OF AMERICA

FFG   10   9   8   7   6   5   4   3   2   1

$\mathcal{F}$OR THE YOUNGS,

THE MOSNYS,

AND THE YOUNG MOSNYS

Acknowledgments

All my love and gratitude to Rudy for the luxury of intellectual space and the necessity of emotional freedom; to Aimi for her fortitude and foresight; to Mathé for his balance and wisdom; to Alaina for her innocence and maturity.

My love to Richard and Melmie for making life entertaining and a caricature.

My gratitude to Wendy McCurdy, my editor, for vision and architecture.

Contents

Chapter One

JUN CHOU, SUCH SHAME

OR WHAT AN ODOR

$\mathcal{S}$he wouldn't listen. She just wouldn't listen.

Ma Ma's face the day long was visiting all shades of gray, a chromatic match for her salt and pepper hair. Between feeling a little dizzy, an uneasiness in every step she took from the waiting room to the examination room, she was feeling less strong, less vital, less *chi*, in her blood. She was hungry, as she always seemed to be, but today she didn't, she couldn't, stop to eat. Eating's importance was never lost on her and hunger disrupted her like a clock every four hours, she actually being one of the proverbial children starving in China. Ma Ma never lost a piece of food on her plate, even on our plates, her children's, and yesterday's leftovers were always highly respected and creatively consumed. Wasting leftovers was equivalent to losing years of your life, she had warned us. Kernels of rice stuck to your bowl will bring you a hideous spouse with pockmocked skin. But today her appetite was only a distant roar, taking a lesser priority, below her eyes, blinking and watery, and her vision, blurred and hazy. Ma Ma wouldn't take the afternoon off. How could she let a little physical discomfort, somehow feeling unnatural, intrude on her purpose, her job, her dedication, as the receptionist and office manager of her son's medical practice? She wouldn't rest.

Leave me alone, she waved her hand. *"Yow ngor."*

Her Chinese words were strong and swift, matching the swing of her head as she turned to look away. She continued to log the names of patients expected to be seen that day.

That night, no, it was predawn, she tried to find her way half in slumber to the bathroom in the Chinatown tenement she had lived in for nearly forty years. Her bedroom was only a few steps away in the four-room apartment, number 12, we had called home as children in the 1950s, on the ground floor of a reddish-brown brick building six stories high, tall enough for a dumbwaiter for garbage but not for an elevator. It sat like a throne in the elbow of Mott Street, the center spine of New York's Chinatown, in the heart of our Chinese ghetto.

Ma Ma had arrived in this Little China as a young bride in 1949, pregnant with my older brother, the doctor, and now she had fallen, struck down by a stroke, an implosion in her brain, exploding her life apart.

And ours.

She had started down the hall in dignity and ended in a pool of urine, where she was to be found the next morning.

. . .

Only ten miles away but a world apart, mornings had been blending into nights and nights into mornings again for me, this time for baby Anni. Every four hours, Anni was awake and looking for her next cuddle at the breast. Snuggling was for me the purest highlight of motherhood. Still, I longed for the day when I could forgo my button-down pajamas for easier nursing and slip back into a silk spaghetti-strap nightgown.

This morning, Monday, was like most school mornings. Anni was my alarm clock, and I in turn was my family's. With Anni in my arms, I scurried to the children's bedroom. My seventeen-year-old daughter, Vicki, was asleep on the top bunk, putting her easily at my height, and I was always happy at some very elementary level that I didn't have to bend down to kiss her. I looked for her nose under the blanket to kiss, and this morning I went to the right end of the bed. Some mornings I ended up kissing her feet because she had fallen asleep at the other end studying where the clip light was. She takes her time to wake up, as do I, so I always kissed her first.

"Two more minutes, Mom," Vicki always said after the first kiss of the morning, pulling the fluffy duvet over her eyebrows. She could have had her own bedroom but a new-found loving, sisterly instinct made her choose to share one with her four-year-old brother.

Mark always jumped out of his bottom bunk every morning, still too short to bump his head, immediately awake, like his father. This morning he put his arms around my knees and pulled us down, Anni and me, and we tumbled into a bundle of rolling, laughing family.

Vicki joined in by swinging her arm down, reaching for us like Dumbo's mother through the gates of jail. We pulled her hand toward us, trying to kiss it. Boy, these kids will require a lot of affection when they grow up.

I managed to pull away with Anni still in my arms as though we were one entity, which we still were in many ways, and stopped for a group hug and kiss with my husband, Tomas, on our way to the kitchen. He leaned out from the bathroom and kept his cheek cocked and taut where he had been shaving and where Anni and I formed a triangle of air with our lips. From the time we were married, Tomas always rush-started his mornings with the loud razz-razz of his electric shaver, claiming he had to shave before our showers steamed up the bathroom. He then rushed to walk Max, our miniature dachshund, before lounging on the sofa with his coffee and the TV morning news. This hurry-up-and-relax routine was his two-step dance every morning.

In our kitchen, which opened out over a long counter into the dining room, I pried Anni away from me, bent her into the high chair, and put a zwieback cracker into her fingers. The view of the Hudson River outside our windows in New Jersey justified the month. Slabs of ice were floating near the shallow slicks of water on our side of the river and the sky was especially thin, I could see from our twenty-third-floor window, making the birds and airplanes appear lighter still. Hot oatmeal. That's what we need this January morning. It was ambitious of me because time usually only allowed for cold cereal. But I could hear help in the barracks. Tomas was trying to convince Mark that wearing jeans would be more comfortable under his snowsuit than wearing sweatpants. Vicki walked into the kitchen in her school uniform, a gray flannel skirt, white turtle-neck, and navy knee socks, looking more grade-school girl than teenager, and immediately started to take milk and juice from the refrigerator to set on the dining table. The blast of cold air from the fridge set me worrying again that her exposed knees would freeze. She squeezed Anni's cheeks together, pursing her lips into fish lips, and gave her a loud kiss. Daughters are wonderful, I thought, but sisters are better, and the phone rang. It couldn't be a snow day, so somebody must need a ride for nursery school.

It was my brother. "Something happened to Ma Ma," Kent said quickly but with pause enough only to try to lessen my shock. I heard his controlled detachment for my benefit. He could have been saying "Today is Monday" with as much emotion, being more the doctor now than the brother or the son. "Ma Ma had a stroke last night and we're taking her to the hospital now."

Stroke.

A brain attack.

That much I knew. But didn't it cripple the body and the brain? Didn't it slur the words and mire the move-ments? Didn't it end life? My shoulder cranked the por-table phone too tightly to my ear as I waited for my brother to explain it magically away like a David Copper-field of Medicine. But instead I saw my hand stirring my stream of warm tears into the pot of hot oatmeal.

"What should I do?" I said, as much to myself as to my brother, becoming in an instant the little sister instead of the mother in charge. How can I get to the hospital be-fore Ma Ma dies? Does Mark really need a snowsuit today?

Will Vicki have to miss her trigonometry exam? How will we ever have time to walk Max? I caught myself in this whirling madness of inconsequential thoughts.

"Meet me at Bankford," Kent said and hung up.

The silence of the still phone gave me a chasm into which the collision of all my thoughts fell. Had I been blissfully breast-feeding Anni in the middle of the night while Ma Ma was suffering a stroke? How damning! My chest began to shake as I put down the phone and my knees buckled in turn. I crouched, my back against the tough, resilient refrigerator door, my hands over my face, the wooden spoon in my hand sticking out of my right ear. The stirring became a tornado in my head. I cannot serve oatmeal with tears to my family, I could not stop thinking. I've got to undo what has been done.

How impossible, how surreal, how pathetic.

Ma Ma, stroke, stillness, paralysis, dying, death.

It was Auntie Win-Da who was this morning kneeling beside my mother in the small square of linoleum hallway where the bedroom met the bathroom. While I was stirring oatmeal, Ma Ma was on the floor waiting for rescue.

Up to the evening before, we had been speaking every other day or so, usually after dinner, by telephone. Ma Ma was immersed in helping to set up my brother's practice as a cardiologist, and I had taken an unofficial sabbatical from a decade-long career as an account manager at an advertising firm. It was time again for more children, time to care for my own growing family in the suburbs. Ma Ma had been the one turning the key to open the office door every morning for the last year. When Kent arrived at the office that morning and found that not only was she not there but the patient list had not been drawn up and the carpet had not been vacuumed, he was annoyed by the inconvenience rather than concerned by Ma Ma's absence.

He briskly telephoned Ma Ma. When no one answered, he called her neighbor, Auntie Win-Da. And so Ma Ma was neither the picture of Asian grace nor American television comedy—"I've fallen and I can't get up"—when her dearest friend and longtime schoolmate was the first to come to her side. Crouching down, Auntie Win-Da stayed calm and authoritative, just as she was in her job as school principal when she told parents their Chinese children had "behavior problems" and were "unteachable." Auntie Win-Da dialed 911 first, then auto-dialed my brother, who called me.

There would be no snow pants for Mark today. It would be a sick day after all, for him, for Ma Ma, for the entire family. We took our family van, bundling Anni into her car seat between Vicki and Mark in the back, and fought heavy morning traffic on the FDR Drive on Manhattan's East Side. We didn't have to listen to the traffic report on 1010 WINS news radio because we were one of the statistics, one of the cars sitting in bumper-to-bumper traffic. Damn, this road has been under construction for the last twenty years. Here's a bottleneck leading to the exit ramp to the Triboro Bridge, another right before Ninety-sixth Street, and still another in the Sixties.

Three lanes have never been open at the same time all the way from northern Manhattan to its southern tip.

"When are they ever going to finish this road? It's just like we're on a Caribbean island!" At least, that was what Tomas and I usually said to each other as we drove to our restaurant in the East Village every day. Today, neither of us said anything.

Today the traffic didn't seem so bad, delaying, as it did, my first sight of Ma Ma. I stared at all the license plates. I played games with the drivers' faces. I felt fear like never before.

We reached Bankford Hospital, just south of City Hall, where my brother at age four had three stitches put in his forehead after a swing smacked him and where I at age eight had my left knee X-rayed after I dashed in front of a moving car. I was a foreigner in a familiar land, stepping back into the neighborhood of my childhood. On warm, humid summer evenings when Chinatown became too stifling with smells of roast duck and tourists from Middle America and garbage of chicken bones, my brother and I indulged our father's idea of after-dinner entertainment: long walks outside the invisible boundaries of Chinatown, south on Park Row from Mott Street in Chinatown to City Hall, sometimes all the way to South Ferry. We skipped over the throwaway boxes with corners bursting with vegetable leaves that restaurant owners were beginning to stack by the curb and sprinted to tap the overhead No Parking signs, reaching for Chinese characters in red and yellow neon as well.

Bankford Hospital was always something formidable and forbidding. Now there weren't even ambulance drivers to distract us with lollipops or nurses with promises of ice

cream afterward. Just an unfriendly policy that barred children from visiting patients. So I had to leave Tomas with
the kids in the hospital lounge and find my way alone to
Ma Ma's fifth-floor room.

I heard Kent's voice even before turning the corner.

"So, you'll be monitoring her closely," he was saying to
the resident in charge.

"Yes, Dr. Liang, we'll take her down for a CAT scan
this morning. We have her stabilized. It looks like a clot,
not bleeding."

"How do you know?" I asked as I walked in. Immediately I felt crowded, assaulted by a gauzy fog of hospital air
and light, of too many people and too sharp a mix of
voices. There were at least six people in the room: the doctor, Kent, Auntie Win-Da, the other patient, and a nurse.
All of them were still, as if afraid to move. I caught sight
of Ba Ba, my father, standing by the wall next to the
window.

"Well, we're guessing right now. The majority of women
her age have ischemic strokes where bloodflow and oxygen
to the brain is blocked by a clot in an artery. Younger
women tend to have bleeding, hemorrhaging," he said.
"You must be her daughter?"

"Yes. How is she?" I meant will she live.

"We're watching her carefully. The first six hours after
a stroke are the most crucial. We're trying to minimize the
damage to the brain cells with drugs. . . ."

I heard little else. He did not say whether she would
live. Or not. That's all I wanted to know.

Ma Ma was on her back, lying in an aluminum-railed,
thin-framed hospital bed that only emphasized her heaviness. Her face was flat against the anemic pillow but swollen

on the left, pulled down by gravity and flattened from the stroke. She looked as though she had just had all of her left quadrant molars and wisdom teeth, upper and lower, extracted by a merciless dentist. She did not speak. Or could not. Just how damaged was her brain? My god, was she a vegetable? She did not move her mouth, a mouth contorted by a penetrating numbness. I imagined that this numbness meant her left lung could not breathe. And her heart, in her left side, did not beat.

Ma Ma was slipping in and out of sleep, or was it consciousness, as I hovered around her, not knowing what to do. She seemed exhausted from the stroke and I searched for her, wondering whether she would pull out of these depths. The fluorescent light in the hospital room painted her hair a yellow white, robbing her of the flattering rose glow of the halogen bulbs my brother chose for his office. Rose lipsticks had always been Ma Ma's favorite, so sexy on her full lips now distorted but still planted like a flower in the bed of her ivory skin. I kissed my sleeping beauty, hoping a child's wish to give her life.

As if through a mist, I heard Kent say he had to leave, his doctor mission done for now, and he offered to take Ba Ba with him. I managed to pull up for enough light and air to say to Kent, "Could you stay with Mark and Anni in the waiting room so Tomas and Vicki can come up?"

No one else sobbed at Ma Ma's hospital bed as Vicki did. She rushed to Ma Ma's bedside, grabbed her hand and sank her head into Ma Ma's stricken left shoulder and cried. Cried that Grand Ma Ma was so ill. Cried that Grand Ma Ma might die. Cried for all of us.

Ma Ma started to cry also, as well as one who has just suffered a stroke could. Her swollen lip ballooned even more; the swelling in her face and throat turned her crying into deep, moaning sounds, more animal-like than human. She had difficulty swallowing, and for a few moments, she almost choked on her tears.

"Vicki, don't cry." These were Ma Ma's first words poststroke, monosyllabic Chinese words. We could hear the thickness, the cloudiness, the effort. It took further concentrated effort to wipe her own tears with the hand that could move, her right.

Ma Ma's choking and crying were a relief. Vicki had brought her back, from how far I don't know. Ma Ma was alive. She pushed Vicki away, dragging the intravenous along with her. "Stand up. Go to school. There's no reason to cry."

"But, Grand Ma Ma, what about you? Will you be all right?"

"If you are all right, I am all right," Ma Ma said, each slur of a word strong evidence of a mind still intact. The words rolled out the loopy corner of her lip, her eyes still closed. She seemed to be meditating. "Study hard. Graduate. Be successful. I want to see you successful."

It sounded like a graduation or deathbed speech. I pulled Vicki away, surrounding her in my arms, trying to be the strongest of the three. Vicki's hand slipped into her father's as they walked away, and for the first time since my brother's phone call, something felt right.

Tomas and I quickly consulted and decided that Ma Ma was right. The kids must go to school, must continue some semblance of their normal routines. At least for today.

I stayed with Ma Ma while Tomas took the children. She was newly exhausted from crying, and a calming, purging sleep came to her, allowing me to study her once again. Her washer-beaten, blue-snowflake hospital gown was too small to go around her round, soft belly. For the rest of the morning and into early afternoon, I tried to keep her warm and covered under the polyester sheet and cotton thermal blanket, both too thin and too small. Each time her arm moved, I feared the intravenous needle would twist out and rip her vein, so I held her hand, trying to keep her arm still. The dripping in the intravenous gave me a steady sign of life, and I untwirled from time to time the plastic tube leading from the hanging plastic bag into the needle to keep the flow free. Ma Ma's chest heaved up and down, but it seemed flat, two-dimensional, more like her face than her rotund belly. She continued to wake periodically, and I worried whether she was slipping into a coma or just simple sleep. She was very drowsy. Was it the drugs or the stroke?

Auntie Win-Da stayed too. I deferred to her today, letting her arrange the chairs in Ma Ma's room, fold her clothes and straighten the closet, making herself quietly busy and worthy, while I sat beside Ma Ma.

Auntie Win-Da was everything Ma Ma had always wanted to be. Besides being a respected educator, she was also a renowned sculptor, painter, and calligrapher. Most of all, she was divorced. She had dared to be in midtwentieth-century America a Chinese working mother without a husband. She had achieved what Ma Ma had never been able to. The final irony would be, I foresaw, when Auntie Win-Da took over Ma Ma's job as office manager for my brother.

By late afternoon, Ma Ma was staying awake for longer

periods of time. There was now a certain sense of organization in the room, each of us settling into the newness. Ma Ma was aware I was touching her as I circled the plumpness around only her middle with my hands and tucked the sheet around her legs, legs that were until today shapely and lean, graceful and balanced. I used to wonder why she didn't tip over. Now I knew. She was in wait for the big one, like Californians, that landed her in this present catastrophe of hers.

But it was not hers alone. I suddenly found myself pulled into the undertow. Peace had left as quietly as it had come. I was wiping her, between her buttocks, and in each stroke, I found myself rubbing in my anger, my denial, my sorrow. No nurse was to be found, and Ma Ma could not wait for the bedpan. As I kept cleaning her, trying to undo what had been done, using one after the other of rough green paper towels, each of my strokes, each pressing harder and longer than the one before, drilled in the questions, why wouldn't she listen? How could she lose so much control? What would we all do now?

All Ma Ma could say was, *"Do je, neuw."* Thank you, daughter. I am, after all, her *cheen gum,* her thousand pieces of gold, her precious only daughter. We Chinese of my mother's generation, you see, often referred to sons with a higher value than daughters, ten times that of daughters, as their ten thousand pieces of gold, their *mon gum.* But Ma Ma never placed a lesser price on me, never made me feel less worthy than my brother. Nor did she discount Vicki or Anni. I was, I am, worth a million to her. Now I could only feel my thousand pieces of tears.

She whispered my name, Jenny, which she always proudly

said means "virginity" in Chinese, a name most eloquent for Chinese girls.

"Jenny, *jun chou*. Jenny, I am so ashamed," Ma Ma hushed out. *"Jun chou. Jun chou."*

"*Jun chou, jun chou*," I repeated to myself. Only my *chou* meant "What an odor!" In Chinese the words to express "shame" and "odor" are both *chou*, a mere difference of inflection, up or down, separating the two.

Late afternoon floated by and evening came heavily. I felt I could do no more, as Ma Ma had done enough. I needed to go home. On the bus threading through the Lincoln Tunnel, I drifted into the darkness. How appropriate, I thought, afraid to look at my own reflection in the window and staring instead into the nothingness. Ma Ma had put us now on this unknown road. My own numbness was behind me, taken over now by an exhaustion that allowed my mind to wander as if in a wakeful dream. I bounced off the sides of our life like a wandering billiard ball, first resisting the idea that Ma Ma's few moments of a stroke could wreck a lifetime, hers and ours; then I was engulfed by a sense of aloneness, feeling as helpless as Ma Ma in her hospital bed.

I reached home as Tomas was frying omelets with large dollops of ketchup and cheese, his specialty, for dinner. They were omelets of whimsy, no two ever alike. How well I knew that sound, the fork poking holes in the eggs and striking the pin-pricked pan. How well I knew that smell, the cheese oozing through and browning. How well I knew that kitchen where only this morning I was stirring oatmeal. How well I knew the expanse in Tomas's eyes after he kissed me hello.

Vicki was playing the card game Uno with Mark and doing her homework at the same time. Anni was fed but not yet breast-fed. I stripped into my pajamas, took Anni to my breast, and went directly to the phone.

I didn't even wait for Kent to say hello. "Did you see Ma Ma tonight? I just got back home."

He was a little breathless, but at least he was home, in his four-thousand-square-foot loft in Tribeca only ten blocks or so from Bankford. Kent had been meticulously renovating this space for years. I could hear the workers in the background, noisily and hungrily putting away their tools. Only Chinese carpenters worked until eight at night, every night. I could sense the urgency over the phone, how the slight, dirty men couldn't wait to eat, not to shower. Food was more godly than cleanliness.

"Yes, I just saw Ma Ma." His voice was husky, like his size. "She's still in critical condition. They're making sure it doesn't get worse, that she doesn't have another stroke. . . ." Kent said. ". . . Okay, good night, thank you! See you tomorrow. . . . What we call a stroke in evolution."

"So what happened? How could this have happened to her?" I moved Anni to the other breast and the phone receiver to the other ear, trying not to miss any of Kent's logical explanation. I was sure he could make sense of our family quagmire.

Kent began to describe somewhat defensively how Ma Ma had looked weak in the office yesterday. She had difficulty focusing and writing. She complained of headache. She wasn't quite herself. "She was feeling nauseated and didn't eat her lunch, and you know how important eating every meal is to her," he said. They were busy, busier than usual, seeing almost double the usual patient load. At six-thirty, after the last patient had left, Kent had been tired and wanted to close up the office.

"Ma Ma, let's go. Dinnertime."

But Ma Ma continued to straighten the office without answering him, tidying the desk, filing the files. As a matter of course, she began to gather the garbage. It was a habit of hers, a bad one at that. She scooped the garbage can from Kent's examination room without stopping and brought it to the waiting room, where she tilted it with one hand and shoved the refuse from one can to the other. This consolidation of garbage was one of Ma Ma's daily chores, and daily, Kent scolded her for this atrocious breach of hygiene. Don't use your bare hands to touch tissues that patients used to blow their nose and cotton pads I used to cleanse the equipment, Kent would tell her, day in and day out. Ma Ma was intelligent enough to know about germs and microbes but too stubborn to pay attention to them.

"How many times do I have to tell you not to do that?" Kent would say, more like a parent than a son. As a doctor, he was not used to his orders being ignored.

Kent asked her three times to leave the garbage, to come with him to dinner. Then he left without her. If only she'd listened to him, he said, he could have kept an eye on her at dinner, watched for any telltale signs that a physiological reason was underlying her physical patina that day, signs he would later explain as TIAs, transient ischemic attacks. These were indicators of a stroke in the making, he said, when staggering and numbness can occur, when words are spoken unclearly or words cannot be found at all.

I heard the guilt in Kent's voice, but did not reassure him. He should not have left her. He was a doctor, damn it. This was his mother. Our mother.

"So was she tired? Overworked?" I said after a moment of accusing silence.

"No, no, Jenny ... it's never as simple as that," Kent said, relieved to be moving back into familiar territory. "It could be a combination of things. Her age, her history of hypertension, her diabetes. But you know how she thinks everything is attributable to hunger: feeling faint, feeling unsteady, feeling tired. There were probably signs that she didn't recognize."

"What kinds of signs?"

"Blurred vision, headache, dizziness, numbness of the arm or leg, or even the face, difficulty talking ..."

"Did she have any of those signs?" I sounded like Ms. Prosecutor trying to establish whether a crime had been committed.

"Not that I knew of. But that doesn't mean she didn't have them."

As we each said good-bye, the phone call felt unfinished. I was suddenly ravenous for Tomas's omelet with splashes of Tabasco sauce. I hadn't eaten since morning. Did I even eat the oatmeal?

Tonight, Tomas ate tortilla chips with grapefruit juice, enjoying it with a childlike gusto like kids who eat sourball candy washed down with cola, grimacing and smiling at the same time. I watched him eat and heard him crunch, and felt an eerie closeness to him. There was comfort in our food, the food Tomas had brought to me at the hospital three times a day when our children were born: chicken enchiladas with miniscoops of guacamole and sour cream; grilled swiss on rye with tomato, toasted dry. The food he had cooked: hot cream of wheat drizzled with honey for breakfast in bed when I was breast-feeding. That night, in bed, before Anni's first night feeding, I felt I had traveled across time zones and heart zones and mind zones, finally finding my way home again into the circle of Tomas's silence and the steadiness of his breathing.

Chapter Two

LOP SOP, GARBAGE

$\mathcal{T}$oday, the second day after Ma Ma's stroke, I wore red. I had learned from Ma Ma long ago that red was for happy days—birthdays, New Year's and holidays, even weddings. Red was for joy. As a girl, I had worn red socks or a red hair ribbon on school exam days to bring me an A, and even now, I never wear total black for evening, a red bra and panties surely underneath.

And today was a day of joy: Ma Ma had not died, after all.

Purposely wearing my swing-cut winter coat with dolman sleeves, I propped Anni on my hip and nestled her under with only the top of her hatted head peering through like a joey. I squeezed silently into the hospital elevator and stared at the blinking lights numbering the floors we passed until we reached five. I knew to turn right immediately when I stepped out, then another right at the end of the hallway to Ma Ma's room, the second door on the left. I had been careful to remember my exact path last night when I left so that when I brought Anni, an unwelcome visitor, I would be able to walk briskly past the nurses' stations and nod like a drill sergeant making rounds.

My brother had once explained to me why doctors made such boisterous, self-important entrances into the rooms of patients. "We don't like to scare patients by sneaking in on them," Kent had said. "We holler because most patients are either old or they're daydreaming, so we announce ourselves, the way a bell announces a cat, only much louder."

But I didn't want anyone to notice Anni, so we glided into Ma Ma's room. Ma Ma was propped up about forty-five degrees in her bed, and today not only did she look less flat, she had more color. Even her hair was less yellow. She opened her lopsided eyes as we entered, and her right hand, her good one, trembled when she lifted it to touch Anni's cheek. We bent down to kiss her, and I breathed in, from my right and from my left, the smell of age and growing old and then the smell of babyhood and growing up. I took in both my mother and my daughter, the different textures of their hair, the temperatures of their skins, the insouciance of their eyes, the history in their voices.

"Why did you bring Anni?" Ma Ma asked. I was startled by the sharp, edgy words in a fast slur, and by the direct look from eyes pulled awry by a stroke.

"I thought you would be happy to see her," I said, feeling oddly challenged.

"So many sick people here," she grumbled.

Here she was, her limp, fat body lying helplessly in bed, and she was still trying to tell me what to do. Imagine that.

"Ma Ma, this is a hospital," I said. Impatience. Already. "It's cleaner here than outside, don't you know that? They're always cleaning." I peeled Anni's hat off her head, the static making her hairs stand on end and dance, then I tried to take her out of her snowsuit, yanking at the zipper, which was catching.

As the zipper gave way, Anni bloomed in her bright berry red sweater matching mine atop a white turtleneck under her corduroy overalls.

Ma Ma's half of a face could not hide all of her pleasure at seeing this Chinese color of joy.

"Good girl, Anni, how pretty you are," she said.

Neither could Ma Ma hide her satisfaction that she had raised a proper Chinese daughter.

Ma Ma and I turned to Anni, who was happy in her innocence and curious to be in this bright harsh place, sitting on my lap next to her Grand Ma Ma, playing with the plastic toy keys I had plucked from my pocket. With a baby blue key jangling in her mouth, she drooled and gurgled.

Now I knew why I had brought Anni, why I had needed Anni with me. She was to be my comrade-in-arms. We were, the two of us, soldiers ready to fight for Ma Ma. Or against her. Whatever it took.

"She's growing so fast," Ma Ma said, almost drooling and gurgling too.

"Yes, she is," I said.

"I don't have *hoong bow* to give to Anni." Ma Ma patted her right hand on the nightstand already cluttered with get-well cards, flowers, and a telephone, almost knocking over the water pitcher. Within the first five minutes of any visit, Ma Ma always gave our children lucky red envelopes, *hoong bow,* with crisp new twenty-dollar bills inside. Tomas and I modernized the tradition, giving Tooth Fairy money in *hoong bows* under their pillows. Ma Ma gave the red packets immediately so as not to forget, and to get business out of the way. It was supposed to bring good luck. We could sure use some today.

"It doesn't matter," I said quickly. "Have you had your breakfast today?" I knew she had eaten but we Chinese asked anyway. We would meet a friend on the street late in the evening and instead of "How are you?" we would ask, "Have you had dinner yet?" The answer would confirm a few things about his status quo: you know at least he's healthy (able to eat) and not penniless (has money to buy food).

"I ate breakfast a long time ago," Ma Ma said. "What about Anni? What did she eat today?" Ma Ma exhaled a big sigh, a sound I had never heard from her, and I noticed the big effort she put into it with half a body paralyzed. As children, we had never been allowed to sigh, for it was considered an expression of grief, and we never had anything to grieve. Until now.

"Oatmeal," I said, sighing myself, remembering my tears in yesterday's oatmeal. What nonsense we were speaking to each other. What a Chinese ostrich game we were playing. Don't say anything bad lest it bring bad luck. "Don't you know? Bad luck comes on the back of bad words. *Dai gut lie see,*" Ma Ma would say to cancel every and any bad omen that leaked from our mouths. Literally, it means: *Wish you a giant, stuffed red envelope, a* hoong bow.

"What would you like me to bring you for dinner tonight?" I asked.

"Nothing. Don't. It's too much trouble," Ma Ma said. "Whatever they have here I'll eat."

What a liar she was. All her life Ma Ma was used to kiwi green soup with chunks of winter melon; slivers of beef steamed with preserved cabbage; poached sea bass with soy sauce, scallions, and ginger; spinach sautéed with bricks of fermented bean curd that were stacked in a glass jar and floated like brains in formaldehyde. These foods were to Kent and me what macaroni and cheese and pizza are now to my children.

Chop, chop, chop.

Ma Ma had prepared dinner every day of our childhood after Kent and I returned from the Wah Kun Chinese Elementary School at 6:00 P.M. and served it promptly at 7:00. *Chop, chop, chop.* I did my homework, both English and Chinese, on the kitchen table covered with a sheet of yellow vinyl that was also Ma Ma's work counter. *Chop, chop, chop.* "Ma Ma, how do you write twentieth century in Chinese?" I would ask. She put down the overweight cleaver and wrote the words, greasing up my pencil. *Chop, chop, chop.* The rice would be cooking in the black-bottomed rice pot seasoned like a French crepe pan, the soup would be simmering in the huge white enamel one, the pork she bought would be pink and lean, waiting on the thick wooden block. *Chop, chop, chop.* Ma Ma seasoned the pork, formed it into a thin patty and spread it out on a plate, breaking a large salted duck egg on top before slipping the dish into the steamer. Each of us would get a quarter of the cooked egg at dinner, and sometimes I even gave mine to Kent.

All the pork. All the salt. Did all the chop-chopping finally strike Ma Ma down?

And now I knew more about making pesto sauce and vinaigrette dressing than traditional Chinese foods. The only way I could bring Ma Ma's favorite foods to her in the hospital was to get takeout from a restaurant. But Ma Ma would catch me faking it.

"Dai gut lai see," I breathed out.

"What did you say?" Ma Ma asked.

"I said, Good luck, Ma Ma." To myself I said, Don't die. Don't give up.

A nurse came into the room, and I quickly pretended I had been zipping up Anni all along and was ready to leave. Ma Ma's temperature needed to be taken and more blood needed to be drawn, medical procedures as foreign to her as the hospital food. Ma Ma was seventy years old, and her generation of women from China was not accustomed to routine checkups, annual Pap smears and mammograms. They only visited doctors when they were too ill to work, and oftentimes not even then.

Ma Ma looked at the nurse, managed to blink her eyes and point her head to the door, signaling for me to go. I left reluctantly, with my heart still by her bedside, just as I did when I left my children on the pediatrician's scale or in the dentist's chair.

"Good morning, Ma Ma." I tried to sound chipper like an office worker facing a week's heavy load of work ahead. It was the third morning after Ma Ma's stroke, and I had figured out how to time my commute to the hospital to catch the lull after the rush-hour traffic and for Anni to start her morning naps in the car. Our visits were becoming routine too quickly, today with Anni continuing her nap in her stroller. The coffee and Danish I had brought for the security guard yesterday and the bright smile today seemed to have worked. I had breezed through the lobby. In Ma Ma's room, I parked Anni by the window even though it was brightest there, and was grateful that the head nurse, too, was understanding enough to let me wheel her in. "I didn't see anything!" she sang out. I was mentally wearing red, but my conquering mood was shattered by Ma Ma's confused air about her this morning, sitting up in bed for the first time. Somehow when she was lying down, it was different. Prone, she had seemed totally helpless, totally accepting of outside forces. But sitting up, she was like a caged bird, so obviously chained by her incapacity.

Still, Ma Ma seemed to have already arrived at a certain resolve. She tried to smile at the orderly mopping the floor. She said "Good morning" to Anni and me with less throatiness. She matter-of-factly acknowledged the nurse who came in to measure her blood pressure. She was even somewhat more expert today in maneuvering a bedpan, anticipating every move made by the nurse's aide. The swelling in her face had shrunk although the droop in her left cheek and jaw still gave her a perpetual frown. Her paralyzed left side was a paradox, simultaneously light and heavy, a stillness like that of an African frog suctioned upside down to a tree branch, resisting the pull of gravity.

"Ma Ma, are you hungry?" I asked. She nodded and reached for my hand. She had been on liquid "food" via the intravenous and only today would she have real food for the first time since the stroke. My question yesterday afternoon was moot after all.

Another nurse's aide, as brusque and crude in her movements as a Chinatown waiter, brought in a tray. It was only about eleven o'clock, but we were on hospital time, and that meant lunch.

The aide shoved the tray onto the small swivel table on wheels beside Ma Ma's bed. I rotated the table to hover over Ma Ma's lap, a lap so limp and indented into the bed, and I lifted the steel cover inverted over the plate.

Chicken pot pie without the pie and mashed potatoes without the gravy. Unsalted bouillon, I guessed, and a lump of cherry gelatin. It may as well have been food from Mars. Ma Ma could never understand potatoes and had never once had instant soup. As for the gelatin, she had made it for my brother and me on occasion in small glass cups when we were able to sneak a box or two into the shopping basket, but she herself has never tasted it.

I tucked the napkin, a green paper towel like the one I had used on the first day to clean Ma Ma, into her collar. The weight of the coarse paper pulled down her flimsy gown.

"I don't need that," Ma Ma protested, trying to use her good hand to swipe it away. Sometimes, Anni did the same. I thought fleetingly of the bib I had tied on Anni that morning, a bib Vicki had bought that read, "If you think I'm cute, you should see my Mom."

"Yes . . . you . . . do," I said, pushing, placing, and tucking the bib in one-two-three cadence.

Ma Ma still tried to twist her neck out from under as I raised a spoonful of soup to my own lips first to test the temperature before gliding it over to Ma Ma's lips. Here comes the airplane.

"What is this?" Ma Ma asked suspiciously. Her nose

got long and her nostrils got big as she looked down at the wobbling spoon.

"Beef soup," I said, dripping the bodiless brown liquid behind her bottom teeth. I was tempted to tip her head back to help her swallow.

"No, it's not. It doesn't taste like beef soup. It doesn't taste like anything."

I tasted it to show her it was just fine. "See, it's good soup."

Ma Ma closed her eyes and shook her head.

So that's how it would be. Ma Ma would be as picky an eater as Anni. Just last night Anni's top lip scrunched up to meet the bottom of her nose, the lower hemisphere of her face smeared with vegetable green, as she had peered suspiciously into the spoon looking for any vegetable I might have tried to camouflage under bitefuls of chicken. If only I could find Ma Ma so adorable or comical.

"Drink it. Drink it anyway. It's good for you," I said, my own voice cloudy now. I wanted to *pour* the whole bowl down her throat. "Drink."

"Enough," she said, pushing my hand away with her good hand. Drips of brown landed on her bib.

My, what a baby. I raised the spoon to her pinched lips. "Eat some more," I insisted. "One more spoonful."

Ma Ma obeyed, just to placate me. But this time, she choked. I hadn't realized how much difficulty Ma Ma might have with the simple act of eating.

Her coughing brought in the nurse, and I hastened to camouflage any mistake I might have made, grabbing the towel off Ma Ma's chest and using it to wipe her lips.

"That's okay," the nurse said. "You can use the napkin as a bib. People who have strokes usually have trouble swallowing. Here, give her some of this gelatin. It's funny, but sometimes they have an easier time swallowing something with a little texture."

I immediately began breaking up the lump of gelatin, relieved to hear the clacking sound of the spoon against the plastic dish. I was ashamed at my impatience with Ma Ma, appalled at my own incompetence. And all I had done was try to feed her.

The nurse tackled the chicken and potatoes for Ma Ma as I looked on. My mother, my daughter. One in a hospital bed, the other in a stroller. Each inhabiting an unfamiliar body, moving with a clumsy preciseness, commanding the body to follow the mind, not always successfully. If I watched too long, my eyes hurt and my mind ached, reeling with images of the woman Ma Ma had been.

Ma Ma had fallen in the night—was it 2:00 A.M., 3:00, 4:00? (no matter)—and found herself lying on the hallway floor, unable to move in the twilight of transition from night to morn and in that twilight of her own mind. Was she awake and really in the nightmare of paralysis? Or was she only dreaming that her left arm and left leg were lifeless? She lay in semidarkness and in semiconsciousness for what were only hours but must have seemed like a lifetime, her life scrolling before her, like a movie out of focus with no sound. She did not know how it would end. She only knew how it began, in China, so far away from the here and now, sometime in 1916 when she was born a girl.

She was the fourth child, and although a girl, Ma Ma was treasured for being the youngest. Two servants, one for her right side and a second for her left, waited on her. Ma Ma's intelligent questions were never pesky, her tireless energy was unmatchable, and her talent for numbers never a target for jealousy. Her father, my Grand Ba Ba, was a pearl merchant and spent most of his time at sea or in Australia where much of his business took him. Every decade or so upon his return to China, he begot another child. And so, there were about nine years between each of Ma Ma's siblings. Such were the bedtime stories I was told. Grand Ba Ba was tall and fair skinned with fingers slender and graceful like a piano player, Ma Ma said. That's why you are tall for a Chinese. That's why you have great cheekbones. And although Ma Ma was a girl, she was sent to school like a boy, studying economics and eventually becoming a banker in Shanghai.

In 1949, fifteen-year-old girls were being matched and married, but Ma Ma refused the concept. She was thirty-one, content as a Chuppie, a Chinese Urban Professional, working for a bank, pretty and slim in her silk mandarin dress with the tall, stiff collar. She had darting dark eyes and smooth hair, cut blunt to her square jaw, and she had great legs. Ma Ma still has great legs.

"I do not want to marry. I cannot leave you," Ma Ma said to her own mother. "Who will take care of you? Who will make sure your rice container is full?"

"You must take care of yourself," my Grand Ma Ma said, her words especially urgent in those years when China was being consumed by the Communists. "You must take this opportunity."

Ma Ma had had many suitors in Shanghai. Mr. Mak, who had holes in the soles of his shoes. He was too cheap or too poor. Mr. Sing, who was too short. A man should have stature. Mr. Fung, who was rich and spent freely. He was a show-off.

"But I will be away from my whole family, you and elder sister and her children. . . ."

"You will make your own family," Grand Ma Ma said. "Go. Don't make me worry about you."

Ma Ma was introduced to Ba Ba, one of many bachelors from America who boasted his GI status when he went shopping for a wife in Hong Kong, in a meeting arranged by mutual friends. She could not find anything about him to criticize. Nor could she disobey Grand Ma Ma or ignore the incoming Communists. I can marry him either in strength or in weakness, she thought. I will be strong, she determined, and sacrifice myself for Grand Ma Ma's peace of mind. I will take a chance—indeed, gamble everything—and venture into a foreign life in a far-away land.

The Chinese say a woman all her life is subservient to a man: the daughter obeys her father; the wife obeys her husband; the widow obeys her son.

Our men—Kent and Ba Ba—entered the hospital room. Ba Ba wandered in behind Kent, clutching a newspaper, and headed in his deliberate slow pace to Anni, who was plucking cereal from a small snack box. Darn! She's eating that sugary and colorful stuff again that Tomas packed. I always pack the plain loops. Can't get it right unless you do it yourself, I was thinking, as I caught Ba Ba midway.

"Hello, Ba Ba." I reached out to kiss his cheek at the

taut muscle where he clenches his jaw under his skin, dry and rough like toast. Kent, who has been closing his office early every afternoon to visit Ma Ma, went to kiss her.

"Hello, Jenny, did you eat yet?" Ba Ba said. "How's Ma?"

"Today she's better. She just ate lunch," I said, knowing him too well to question the newspaper or wonder why he didn't go to Ma Ma and ask her himself. Instead he went to Anni, looked down through the lower half of his bifocals, brushed her head and smiled.

Then Ba Ba planted himself in the orange molded plastic chair next to her stroller.

A nurse came in to give Ma Ma a white pill from a small plastic cup. It was almost impossible for her to swallow, and as she gagged, the sound coincided with the snapping sound of Ba Ba's newspaper unfolding. The headline of the *New York Post*, I could see, read, "A Mountain of Garbage: Strike Goes into Eighth Day." Below the headline was a half-page photo of black plastic garbage bags at least ten bags wide by four bags high stacked in front of an Upper East Side luxury co-op.

I thought of our own mound of family garbage, our own *lop sop*, neither luxurious nor neatly bagged. It was *lop sop* that had brought us all here, the garbage that Ma Ma had insisted on handling the night of her stroke, the past each of us never threw out.

I tried to see Ba Ba past the front page, but all I could see was our own *lop sop*. I longed for Ba Ba to sit at the side of Ma Ma's bed, to hold her hand and to look into her eyes the way husbands do on television commercials for insurance companies.

"Why do you always have to do that?" I said, suddenly furious. First the soup, now the newspaper.

Ba Ba flipped his newspaper down and toward him, the top edge cutting at his neck. He looked at me as though his ears were cupped or my tongue were foreign.

I saw the shadow of the few wisps of hair on top of his head glowing in the window light. I wanted to yank them out, to pull Ba Ba like a puppet into some sort of action.

"Let him do what he wants," Kent said evenly.

"Like how you let Ma Ma do what she wanted? With the garbage?" My voice was cranked, the pitch high.

"What are you trying to say?" Kent stayed calm.

"Maybe you should have insisted. Maybe you should have better control. . . ."

Ma Ma was making motions with her good hand for me to be quiet. Why did I think all of a sudden I was the commander in chief of the Liang Family Emotion Department?

"Ma Ma needs all of us now," I continued fiercely.

"Let it go, Jenny." Kent was amazing. "She's doing fine just the way it is."

I turned to Ba Ba, staring at him, daring him to act. Or at least speak.

He did. "Look what she did to herself," Ba Ba burst out, "to *me*, to you two, to all of us. So stupid!"

Ba Ba stood up, almost jumping out of the chair, and walked out of the room, all of a sudden in fast motion. Kent said, "If you're so smart, *you* take care of it," and followed him out the door. Anni stopped eating her cereal. Ba Ba went home, not even folding his newspaper, and I was left staring at an empty orange chair.

•   •   •

They say the fire was caused by Mrs. Choy pouring hot oil down the incinerator chute, what Kent and I liked to call the Dumb Waiter. Mrs. Choy had been deep-frying puffy sesame pastries after dinner to bring in a fat and fluffy Chinese New Year in their fourth-floor apartment of our tenement building. At nine years old, I didn't believe anyone would be stupid enough to dump oil down the dumbwaiter. But my brother insisted someone else's cigarette, probably Old Man Lee's on the top floor, tossed down the chute after the hot oil must have sparked the fire.

I remember Mrs. Choy screaming, "*Ai ya! Gow mang ah!* Save my life!" but my brother remembers Mr. Choy clopping down the stairs and turning right at the front door down Mott Street probably to pull the red fire alarm on the corner where Pell Street intersects with Mott. Well, at least he didn't pull the mail box. New Chinatown residents often confused the red fire-alarm boxes with the blue mailboxes where they slipped envelopes with American dollars to start their journey to relatives in China. False alarms were very, very common.

It was also the week of celebrations for the Chinese New Year, and the sound of firecrackers mixed with the smell of gunpowder heightened the sense of danger. Perhaps that is why the stomping of gigantic firemen in oversized yellow slickers and black rubber boots carrying water hoses and axes pointing at us through our front door was so terrifying. Far below, we could see my father's frozen figure.

Ba Ba had been out that evening as usual, after dinner, probably to watch a mah-jongg game at the Pretty & Fragrant Noodle Factory. Like many other factories, Pretty &

Fragrant served as an after-hours game room for men. Once the machinery stopped and all fluorescent work lights were turned off, the card table was pulled out under a lone incandescent lightbulb and real "work" began. When the news caught up to Ba Ba that our building was on fire, he rushed home—not to rescue us, but to go around the block to the parking lot on Mulberry Street from where he could get a better view.

We could see him standing down there for what must have been three hours as Kent and I sat dangling our feet from the windowsill waiting to be saved. Ba Ba stood about twenty feet from the bottom step of the fire escape, his arms crossed around his chest and his head under a felt Stetson hat, tonight the black one. Meanwhile, Ma Ma was trying to fight her way past the firemen and their paraphernalia down the front hall from the store to us.

Ma Ma lost her voice the following day, from screaming to us and from inhaling the smoke and gunpowder. We expected her to lose her voice on every Chinese New Year thereafter, and many years she would disappoint us but some years she did not. We also lost our front door, which the firemen clawed down with their axes. In the end, the fire was pretty much contained in the incinerator chute. On each floor, only the brick surrounding the incinerator door was charred, the black forming halos of smoky stars.

Kent and I cased the damage the next day, stepping over debris peppered with red shreds of firecracker paper in the hallways and stairwells. He liked the shape of the charred star on the fourth floor most; I voted for the one on the sixth floor. In the aftermath, the fire did not seem serious enough for the search-and-destroy mission the firemen had undertaken. But still, it was Ma Ma who came through with her cloth shoes wet from the water and cut from the broken glass to pull us in from the fire escape and it was Ma Ma who was shaking in her cloth shoes for weeks to come.

After that, I waited every night standing by our front door, peering down the fireman's hall, for Ma Ma to come home after closing the shop before I felt safe enough to sleep.

Here in the hospital, I still wait.

Ba Ba was born the youngest of nine children in the Liang family, all from the same mother, all sisters before him—a statistical miracle in China six years after the turn of the twentieth century. Named Hang Chung, meaning "walk strong," he was a wiry boy taut as wrought iron, but suffering from constant nosebleeds and what today would be diagnosed as asthma. The family blamed his tenuous hold on life on his special station of being the only son and on his unusual wavy hair with a cowlick at his right temple.

Taking no chances, his mother brought him to a *feng-shui* man, a wind-water fortune-teller, what my brother in current high-tech lingo calls the "geo man," the one who merges the natural elements—the earth, the stars, the spirits, the human—into one entity, fusing their beings and placing all in order. *Feng-shui* spirits, living or dead, inhabit a place and bring a person the four corners of well-being: happiness, fortune, longevity, and peace. We apply *feng-shui* in life or in death, in the past or in the future, with the perfect birth said to be into the right family, a good life void of any strife, culminating in an even better death prior to the ultimate burial on a high mountain with tall trees and a view of water.

The geo man felt Ba Ba's hands and looked into his palms, pressed the shape of his head like a cantaloupe, had him shake fortune sticks. He researched the calendar, he calculated Ba Ba's date of birth, he reviewed the family up and down. Ba Ba could not live up to the prominence of being the only son, the geo man said, by living in China.

"Your son's life is too much at risk here," warned the geo man. "He must live far away to live long."

Ba Ba's mother let the spirits have their way, a lost son better than no son, feeling the red essence of her blood replaced by ghostly white, feeling the line between happiness and sadness never so blurred. And so, at age fourteen, this prized only son was shipped to America, leaving his doting sisters for a small, closed bachelor society, a community of old men living in New York's Chinatown. Ba Ba arrived in 1920, a year when only sixty-two thousand Chinese lived in the United States.

Ba Ba had been shipped off like an aristocrat but came to live like a pauper, expelled from one unwelcoming place to live in another. With only one suitcase of tattered brown leather framed with metal triangular corner reinforcements, Ba Ba landed feet-first in the Mott Street tenement he would live in for most of his life.

It was a time when discriminatory federal, state, and union rules barred Chinese from many jobs, including civil service and teaching, medicine and dentistry, and some manufacturing jobs. Thus, many Chinese men resorted to opening their own laundries and restaurants. Ba Ba was told he would be safe when he arrived in America within the Chinese clan, the associations that linked people together by name or by village, just like at home. But it was a time of tong wars between associations, of gambling houses behind the barbershop tucked in basements of buildings in slivers of winding streets, of a world run by old men with short brushy hair and musty smells, hands encased in dark crackly skin, fingers looking like cigars. There was no woman's touch, no perfume in the air, no embroidered lace doilies under lamps, no flowers in vases, no slim fingers plucking a lute.

The fourteen-year-old Ba Ba moved in with a Mr. Chin and a Mr. Lee. He ran errands and did chores for his room and board. He busied himself with learning the new ways and the new language. He went to evening English classes for "mountain cows," what the older Chinese immigrants were called who were just learning their ABCs. But much of his new country's language Ba Ba absorbed catch as catch can, on the streets, from the old men, in the shops, in the mah-jongg parlors. The dialects were many, just like in China where peoples living on opposite sides of a river or mountain spoke different dialects and could not understand each other.

Nearly every afternoon, Mr. Chin and Mr. Lee readied themselves for the woman visitor, washing their hands and body and face, shaving with a straightedge razor after brushing up a lather with cream, throwing on lime aftershave lotion, threading Brylcreem into their hair with all ten fingers. Ba Ba was then sent out of the apartment almost every evening to wait on the steps facing the street at the front door, in the rain or in the snow, in the heat or in the cold, while this prostitute or that came to visit Mr. Chin or Mr. Lee.

"Go out now," Mr. Chin or Mr. Lee would say to Ba

Ba. "We'll call you later to come in." Sometimes it would not be until 2:00 A.M. when Ba Ba was allowed back into the apartment.

Among his errands, Ba Ba's most favorite was fetching the newspapers. He bought two, just as he would do for my current-events homework, one in Chinese and one in English. He read the English newspaper forward and backward, again and again, while waiting on the steps. The sports news and stock market reports, neither of which were ever in the Chinese papers, didn't particularly attract Ba Ba's attention. He tried to understand all the words, which surprisingly was easier than pronouncing them correctly, constantly cross-referencing with a Chinese-English dictionary.

Ba Ba and his newspapers came to be inseparable.

From behind the nightly newspaper Ba Ba had told his stories to Kent and me. Incidentally. By the way. He would be reading about President Johnson and civil rights, flip the corner of his newspaper down and glance over to me as I was writing my current events report. We bought two papers every evening after dinner, the *Daily News* and the *New York Post*, and I would take one to do my homework and Ba Ba took the other.

"You know," he'd start, sometimes totally behind the paper, as though he were using the newspaper as notes, "we Chinese had a hard time, too. When I came to America, people thought China was backward and so were Chinese. China was poor, they said, and Chinese ate rice and rats.

"They started by taxing the Chinese workers with a foreign tax," Ba Ba said. "Then Chinese citizens could not vote, could not testify in court, could not even go to public schools. We were considered second-class people like the blacks and the Indians. There were anti-coolie leagues like the Ku Klux Klan. Even a judge said that we were inferior, you know, intellectually, and we were different, different in language, opinion, color, and the way we look. It was okay for Chinese to come to America and only work, not to put down roots."

Listening to Ba Ba, it was like the news coming alive. As Ba Ba did.

Chapter Three

CALM HEART

$\mathcal{D}$uring the first week at the hospital, the expected coterie showed up, all those relatives and friends you never see except at weddings or funerals. And then they faded away as inexplicably as they had come. Auntie Win-Da and I came and went, bringing Ma Ma fresh pajamas, underwear, and perfume samples from home, buying travel-size baby shampoo and toothpaste. Every day after getting Vicki and Mark off to school, I headed for the hospital with Anni to get a reading on Ma Ma's status quo. It was like getting the weather report, the overnight highs and lows. I braced for the forecast, trying to interpret the cautious words of the resident on duty reading from the chart.

"Your mother is doing very well, considering her age."

Did that mean she would "do" better if she were younger?

"Your mother can recover some movement on her left side, if she is motivated and determined. She will have to work with a physical therapist."

How much movement? What did he mean by motivation and determination? Was she really that much in control?

"Your mother should be careful about what she eats, especially her salt and sugar intake, because of her hypertension and diabetes."

Hadn't she been careful enough? Was the stroke her own fault?

Had she created this catastrophe in all our lives?

I listened to the doctors and tried to read between the lines. I struggled to process this information for myself and to translate it to Ma Ma. I wanted her to have hope but not misguided hope. She was after all living within her physical self with an intimacy only she had with her new, unable body.

Early one morning, Auntie Win-Da stopped by to see Ma Ma before going to work. She was leaving just as I was coming in with Anni. I took this opportunity to formally thank her, ready to get on my knees and kow-tow three times, for all she had done. I held Auntie Win-Da's hand in my left, and I held Ma Ma's in my other.

"Auntie, I want to thank you for saving Ma Ma," I said, "thank you with my hottest of hearts, as the Chinese say."

"No, Jenny, you don't have to thank me. It is my obligation."

Boy, that's something you can't write in a greeting card.

It was my obligation now. "And thank you, Auntie, for helping Kent, for taking Ma Ma's place."

"Being able to help brings me happiness." Auntie Win-Da's hand was bony in mine, as rigid as her speech, forever the lady principal.

I felt Ma Ma's hand flinch, her hand gripping mine.

"Yes, I thank you too, Win *jeah jeah*. You are to me more like a blood sister," Ma Ma said. "Take care of my son."

Auntie Win-Da left for her new job as Kent's receptionist. She was busy with a new importance, an importance that had once been Ma Ma's. I slipped my vacated hand over Anni's small and delicate one, a hand I knew so well from holding while breast-feeding, a hand I didn't let go even while she was napping. This little hand was now pulling me for a walk. I hunched down and together we made some circuits around Ma Ma's bed like sentry guards. Ma Ma's eyes followed us.

They were incongruous twins: Anni, relishing the novelty of new movements in her quick-growing body, while Ma Ma, once swift and busy, struggled to move her own heaviness through air as thick as fast-setting cement. Anni delighted in pulling herself up onto her feet at the sides of her crib, climbing onto chairs, kitchen counters, and her car seat. They both struggled with learning to speak words, to form sounds with meaning. The left side of Ma Ma's face, the numbness in cahoots with her paralysis, often interfered. She strained to talk and we strained to listen. Anni babbled and made sounds that resembled "ma" or "da."

Who would have thought that I'd have two in diapers at the same time—my seventy-year-old mother and my year-old daughter?

In the past week, Anni had become clingy and insecure,

fighting with Ma Ma like a sibling for my attention. That night after dinner, Tomas asked me to go for a walk with him. We had just eaten ham and scrambled eggs on top of rice drizzled with soy sauce for the kids and red pepper flakes for us.

"No, I can't. I'm really tired," I said.

Tomas went out alone, taking Max with him. I put Mark and Anni into the tub together and read them two stories, *Alexander's Bad Day* for Mark and *The Cat in the Hat* for Anni. We continued with *We're Going on a Bear Hunt* in bed when Tomas returned. Gathering us into his arms, he kissed each of us in turn goodnight. I felt his kiss rimmed with the chill of a black night.

I realized I missed Tomas. I missed our life before Ma Ma's stroke. I missed our nightly walks, walks we had taken regularly since the beginning, the beginning of us. Walks that at first I had resisted because they reminded me too much of those childhood walks to City Hall and South Ferry that Ba Ba had insisted upon. I had not wanted this man I had married to be a walker like Ba Ba.

Even with all the kids asleep and the whir of the dishwasher long gone, I could not go to Tomas. He gave me hugs I could not hug, kisses I could not kiss. I needed him, but I found our intimacy at once too crowded and too vast.

"Jenny," Tomas said, wrapping his arm around my middle where there was no belly like Ma Ma's. "I know this is all pretty hard on you."

His words were too rational. He didn't know about rough green napkins and drippy brown soup, about great legs and rosy lips, about bony hands and baby hands. I lifted his arm, surprised at how big and heavy it was compared with the arms I had grown to know: Ma Ma's, Auntie Win-Da's, Anni's. "You just don't understand," I said, pushing his arm away. My god, I was becoming Ma Ma.

Tomas was undaunted. "Jenny, you've got to prioritize," he said gently. "You and the kids come first, then Ma Ma. . . ."

His words infuriated me. "This is not a business." I was shrill. "I can't put a rank on everyone. Everyone counts! Everything matters!"

"But you're taking everything too personally, too emotionally . . . you have to stop feeling that you have to control everything."

I hated hearing this. It felt like criticism. It was criticism. This on top of everything. "If I don't, no one will." My fear was a runaway train. "If I don't do it, no one does."

"Jenny, you're spreading yourself too thin. You've got to delegate. You can't do everything yourself. Even Anni is suffering from it—she wakes up six times a night now. You've got to let go a bit. . . ."

"Leave Anni out of it. I'm fine. I'm there if Ma Ma needs me. I'm there if the kids need me. I'm there if you—"

"You really think so? You really think you're here right now?"

I was saved by Anni's crying. I went to her, lifted her out of the crib and hugged her, squeezing too tightly for her to stop crying. Panting, I couldn't give her the breast.

"Well, you're not here all the time either!" I turned on Tomas. "You spend most of your time in the restaurant. And when you come home you're exhausted, too. Too exhausted to do anything. You even spend more time with Max!"

This was insane. Imagine being jealous of our dog.

As I sank into sleep, I hated them all—Kent for not taking Ma Ma to dinner; Ba Ba for reading his newspapers; Auntie Win-Da for her frail, competent hands; Tomas for pretending to understand when he didn't understand anything; and most of all Ma Ma for being sick.

Perhaps if Dr. Cheng were still alive, Ma Ma would never have fallen that night.

Every afternoon, as regularly as the dusty platform truck delivered the wooden-slat crates of live chickens to the poultry market on Worth Street around the bend from Mott, Ma Ma had visited Dr. Cheng. Dr. Paul Kuo-Ming Cheng. Ma Ma called him K.M. On the corner of Mott and Bayard, above a store that sold cold pickled pig's feet with a sweet-and-sour dip only in the summertime, up a narrow, carpeted winding staircase that was the classiest in Chinatown, Dr. Cheng's waiting room on the second floor was always dark and cool, the only light coming from the small tropical fish tank in the corner. The ceiling lights were never turned on. He used the natural light pouring into his office to look down our throats when they were sore. We looked up as he looked down through his eyeglasses. But he raised his eyes to the ceiling as he lifted the needle to pump out the air bubble before injecting our backsides with immunizations and flu vaccines. You could never see Dr. Cheng's eyes because his smile made them into slits, unlike Ba Ba's whose eyes stayed wide open with few laugh lines. Dr. Cheng's head was balding, which,

I deduced, was why he lived in the rich suburban town of Baldwin, Long Island. To us, Dr. Cheng was like a fairy godfather.

Sometime during a weekend visit to Dr. Cheng's big house when Kent and I were preschoolers, Ba Ba got the idea into his head that the doctor was being too good to Ma Ma. Maybe it was the mohair wool throw Dr. Cheng brought to her out of concern that she was cold. Maybe it was the food he brought to her plate with the top end of his chopsticks during each of several dinners. Maybe it was simply being in Dr. Cheng's house, a house with a garden and a driveway.

For her part, Ma Ma had taken note of how obliging Ba Ba was to Mrs. Cheng, this Chinese woman more autocratic than submissive, more square than oval. He helped her carry vegetables in from the garden. Then he helped her wash the greens, side by side in the kitchen. Ma Ma saw the hand soap fall into the sink full of lettuce and water.

At dinner Ba Ba said, "This salad tastes very good to the mouth. *Ho ho sik.*" And then Ma Ma watched him eat the last leaf covered with soapy dressing. She hoped it would bubble up and choke him.

He had never said *ho ho sik* about Ma Ma's no-nonsense cooking. Neither did he say in so many words that it didn't taste good. Instead, he would approach the dinner table armed with the long-spouted can of peanut oil and drizzle thin streams of infinity loops over the Chinese broccoli or mustard greens that Ma Ma had just sautéed and placed on the table. My brother and I swallowed his fancy wristwork in silence.

After that weekend, Ba Ba forbade Ma Ma to see Dr. Cheng. So once a week, usually on Friday around two o'clock before our dismissal from school, Ma Ma secretly hurried away for a "routine checkup." Dr. Cheng eventually diagnosed Ma Ma's hypertension, after which she went daily to have her arm wrapped and pumped to check her blood pressure. Don't let me die, she prayed daily. Yet.

"Ma Ma, how is your blood pressure?" I asked after each visit.

"I'm fine, everything's fine," she always replied. "I'm just nervous about seeing Dr. Cheng secretly. That's why I have high blood pressure."

She came home from Dr. Cheng with what she called "a calm heart." Dr. Cheng also prescribed an after-dinner potion bottled in dark brown glass. Ma Ma drank a tablespoon every night before washing the dishes, holding her breath and saying in a nasal voice, "Just in case I have high blood pressure." He took care of all of us—Ma Ma, Kent, and me—without ever charging a fee. Ma Ma brought him gifts on holidays, red bean moon cakes on the Harvest Moon, sticky rice stringed in pouches of olive drab leaves on the May Fifth Festival, a handknit maroon scarf on Christmas.

And when Dr. Cheng died, Ma Ma's calm heart died with him.

Chapter Four

DAI GUT LAI SEE,

GOOD LUCK

Tomas leans down to kiss Ma Ma, changing the angle of light which brings out the darkness and lines under his eyes. He says he's not tired. But the night before, Tomas managed the night shift at our restaurant again, closing at two o'clock in the morning and not leaving until three when all the staff had checked out. He arrived home, his hair smelling of cigarettes and his clothes smelling of hot frying oil, but right after his shower, the telephone rang with a call from the police: the alarm at the restaurant had gone off, which meant either a burglary or a clumsy cleaning staff. Tomas pulled on his jeans again and drove downtown. He stayed in the city and met me at Bankford.

"How are you feeling this morning?" he asks Ma Ma. She doesn't seem to mind the kiss; I even see her move her cheek expectantly. But she is jostled when Tomas reaches for her hand and holds it. He has never held her hand before.

"I am good," she says. "And you?" She is trying to squirm her hand out of his. "How is business?" She was always trying to distract him.

Then, to me in Chinese, she says, "Tell him not to hold my hand."

"Leave it," I command in a whisper. "Let him."

Ma Ma closes her eyes. The Chinese ostrich game again.

Before Tomas can answer, I am jumping down her throat. "You're unbelievable, Ma Ma!" I grab Tomas's hand out of hers. "After all these years, you still can't see."

Ma Ma keeps her eyes closed.

"Even when you're half-paralyzed you can't see beyond your grudge. Tomas is a much better husband than you ever had!"

"Jenny, don't worry about it," Tomas says quickly, catching on. "It doesn't bother me. I understand."

He picks up Ma Ma's hand and kisses it, while still holding mine.

When World War II interrupted Ba Ba's life, he had already managed a high school diploma, had traveled north to see Boston and south to see Washington, D.C. He had even acquired his U.S. citizenship.

The war gave him the chance to show off his American citizenship by enlisting with Uncle Sam. Hard labor lacked aesthetics and hard fighting was for younger men, but Ba Ba discovered a visual niche as an X-ray technician, which he enhanced with a pocket camera. Our family album was filled with photos of his army buddies. Kent and I used to play games with the faces in the group pictures of the U.S. soldiers in their green wool army uniform and slim triangle of a hat. "Look at this guy," Kent would say, pointing. His soldier had big ears. "Look at *this* guy," I tried to top him. My soldier had a big nose. "*This* guy looks like he's got sand in his butt," Kent would say. "*This* guy looks like he can't get a wife," I would say. We searched for Ba Ba's face among them, and sometimes found him. One photo of him—a self-portrait he had taken with a tripod—in a suit and tie, wavy hair parted in the middle, teeth broad and strong widening his upper lip into a grimace of a smile, has always stood propped next to our childhood television set.

Coming out of the army with the cachet of a veteran, Ba Ba at the age of forty-three was finally ready to take on a wife. He made his way to Hong Kong in early 1949, and through friends of friends became the gentleman caller at the villa of my Yee Ma, Ma Ma's older sister. Ma Ma, single and working in a bank, was living with Yee Ma and her husband and their seven children, who quickly became the conduit for Ba Ba's courtship of Ma Ma.

"Come. Let's go kite flying," Ba Ba invited Yee Ma's two youngest, the boys. Chinese kite flying was as homespun as American baseball, with weekly competitions like ballet in the skies among exquisite works of art and physics. The kites were not only artistically ingenious butterflies and birds and dragons and insects, but they were also dangerous cutting instruments in kite fights with glass-chip-embedded strings pulled taut in the wind to destroy the competition. The stunts were impressive—figure eights and dogfights with just a twitch of the string. Some kites never ascended, others were lost to treetops, but those that soared seemed to be in a mating dance, flirting and charming in their moves, until only one victor commanded the skies.

Yee Ma's four-story villa on the peak overlooking the harbor was white stucco with a grand staircase winding up to the front door. A lichee tree in the backyard strung with lanterns was the anchor of many a garden party for the elite of Hong Kong. It was also the tree around which family and friends, as many as fifty in one sitting, gathered for photographs: the women in narrow, upright pastel silk dresses seated in front, crossing their slim, pale legs all in one direction; the men standing in back with dark robes and mandarin collars and no smiles; the boys in white shorts, white shirts, black suspenders, and neckties; and the girls in flowered, smocked English dresses, all gathered on the grass in front. There was always a ghost of a girl in these pictures: Ying, the fifth daughter of Yee Ma's, who died young. Depending on whom you asked, she died at age four or age nine, of natural causes or at the hands of a servant. "Don't ask about her." Ma Ma shoved us whenever we did. *"Dai gut lai see."* Ma Ma was so afraid we would die too.

Actually Yee Ma's high-society aura was a facade. The villa had been rented. The servants and the cooks and the "milk nannies," some twenty at a time, were not Yee Ma's personal workforce but were in the employ of the government. Yee Ma's husband, Yee Jeung, wore fine suits and carried a cognac in one hand and a Dunhill cigarette in the other, but he was a diplomat in limbo, whiling away his time in Hong Kong waiting for the future.

But Ba Ba thought he had waltzed into a Hong Kong "age of innocence."

My two boy cousins were entranced with Ba Ba. Every day he visited, a Stetson on his head, a newspaper under his arm, a newspaper that was a Hong Kong daily written in English. Every day, he took them kite flying, leaving Ma Ma at home to sew or to knit sweaters for my cousins or to go over their homework. It was a remote courtship, but it worked: what could be a better choice for a husband than a well-to-do Chinese man from America with a kindness toward children, Yee Ma said. The Chinese Communists were descending and the mood was darkening. Ma Ma would be safe in America.

Ba Ba thought he had plucked a flower from a luxurious and fantastic garden. He expected his wife to pack her wealth into her suitcases and carry them to him, to somehow make up for the little he himself had brought when he emigrated. Their wedding was simple and civil, Ma Ma's wedding photo serving double duty as her passport picture.

Ba Ba returned to the United States immediately after their wedding and sent for her once immigration officials approved her entry.

Ma Ma left Hong Kong, already pregnant with my brother. The flight—the first of her life—was by way of Calcutta, a city so dusty and dirty, crowded and poor, that she vomited for the three nights of the layover and worried that this was a disastrous omen for her marriage. Her journey ended with three nights on Ellis Island, where she signed the immigration documents "Lilian Eng Liang," keeping her maiden name as her middle name.

When Ma Ma stepped out of the taxi and looked up at the tall solemn buildings of Chinatown, Ba Ba waited, as he had always done, on the front steps. They walked, he in front and she behind, straight in to the apartment where she would decades later have a stroke.

His first words to her were: "What did you bring?"

"Only these two suitcases," Ma Ma had said, proud of her ability to travel light. For a moment, Ba Ba imagined the two suitcases filled with nothing but money. But they seemed too heavy to be carrying bills and too light to contain coins.

"Why did you bring so little?" he asked.

"I don't need much," Ma Ma said. Ma Ma has never needed much. "I brought just a silk comforter and some clothes."

"What did Yee Ma give you?" Ba Ba persisted.

"The silk comforter."

Ma Ma did not yet understand. She did not yet see the kites flying overhead: colorful and artful flight to the outsider's eye but cunning and cutting to the insider's heart. One flew high while the other flew low. One leaned west when the other leaned east. The wind was too strong for one, not strong enough for the other.

At first, Ma Ma supported Ba Ba in his new career, pushing me in a stroller with Kent standing on the wheel axles to meet Ba Ba after night school at the Hiller School of Photography in the basement of a building opposite City Hall. Only the harsh lights and the pungent photo solutions could break the grinding trip, the grating noise of the cement sidewalks too close to my ears and the sharp bumps too hard on Kent's young knees. Something robust came from Ba Ba behind a full-size-negative Rolleiflex. He seemed to have found his calling as a professional photographer. All these men in Chinatown, after all, needed to send photographs home to China.

"See, look at these men. They had it hard," Ba Ba once said, catching me going through his large matte black box of duplicate photos. "We men were alone. No women. See, this is really the Moy family, but Ho took it and made it his." The photo of husband and wife seated and son and daughter-in-law standing had been delicately cut and pasted, the heads scissored out and replaced with new ones slightly askew. It looked like a circus farce, the weakling's head atop the strong man's body, the beautiful face atop the fat lady's neck.

"Why did he do this?" I asked.

"Ho's wife was still in China, and so was his son's wife. But he wanted a portrait of the family together. So he made one. Lots of my customers did this, pretended the family was together when the wives were still in China."

Ba Ba was luckier than the others. He and his wife and children really were together, not just a mirage of a family, a collage of photo scraps pasted together. Unlike the other "Chinamen," Ba Ba did not become a cook or a waiter or a laundryman or a barber. He opened a photo studio, called it The Natural Studio, and moved his family over to live in one side of the apartment. He converted the living room into the waiting room where his children played and his clients sat. The kitchen became the darkroom, and one of the two bedrooms became the studio with an octagonal backdrop of teakwood to frame each portrait. From under the black shroud behind the camera, Ba Ba spoke openly and animatedly to his subjects as he set up each shot.

Ma Ma chopped vegetables and meat on the three-inch-thick wooden board in the kitchen around his picture trays. Kent scooted around Ba Ba's tripods, throwing balls at pictures hanging up to dry. I crawled and chased behind.

"Ai, deem ho ah?" Ma Ma muttered and muttered. *Chop, chop, chop.* "What can we do?" *Chop, chop, chop.* "One day his bottles of photo solution will poison us all!"

Still, Ma Ma managed to keep an eye on us toddlers and managed the business side as well. She put everyone ahead of herself, spending money budgeted for the household on fresh fruit for Kent and fresh fish for Ba Ba. She gave Kent one prized fillet cheek of the sea bass and me the other while Ba Ba picked at the tenderest tail. She ate last, finishing up in the kitchen, and often ate what we left behind, sometimes mostly the sauce mixed with rice. She bought new dresses for me and new hats for Ba Ba. She wore what Ba Ba would no longer wear, his prickly, mannish jackets and cardigans, the sleeves always rolled up. But the money wasn't enough, so when the three-hundred-square-foot store at the street level of our tenement became available, Ma Ma and Ba Ba took it on and opened a gift shop selling porcelain vases, ivory figurines, wooden chopsticks, and plastic souvenir toys. Ba Ba began to spend less time behind the camera and more and more time strolling along Mott Street and chatting up the news with his acquaintances or watching the local mah-jongg game. He took over the shop for the hour Ma Ma cooked dinner, watching the store from across the street while talking with the shop owner. He occasionally rearranged the display window.

Ma Ma was losing ground, trapped in a single dimension, a flat space too narrow for her existence. The shop became her husband; she indulged in it every day of the year, especially on Christmas and Labor Day. She was invariably the first on Mott Street to open shop in the morning. *"Jo sun, ah moo,"* everyone said on their way out of Chinatown via the subway on Canal Street—"Good morning, ma'am"—as Ma Ma swept the sidewalk, the pebbly gray concrete squares full of tourists' debris from the night before. She even kept aside a special pair of old dirty shoes she wore just for sweeping. Ma Ma didn't have to sweep New York City property but she did, feeling that all of Chinatown belonged to her.

For thirty years, Ma Ma was her own boss. She diligently stayed open late, usually till midnight on Saturday nights in hopes that some late-night shopper would buy a vase for fifty dollars. She had had enough sales of ten-cent chopsticks and five-cent postcards. Ma Ma ran the store, accounting for every penny earned and spent, tearing open the large cartons when weekly shipments arrived and hand shredding the boxes to condense the garbage, the *lop sop*. She raised my brother and me in the middle of it all, giving change to customers with one hand and supervising our homework with the other. In the shop, using her knees as a desk to do my homework every afternoon between three and four o'clock, when I was shipped off to the Wah Kun Chinese Elementary School, I half listened to past pieces of her life. How she had dodged bullets during World War II, actually feeling the metal pellets whiz past her legs. How she had blackened her face and soiled her hair, passing as an old hag to avoid being raped when she traveled by boat to visit her mother in the mountain village. How difficult it was for her to say, even now, "made in Japan" and how she could never ever eat sushi. How men had courted her but how she had needed no man. Her stockinged foot, in thick, beige support hose, pressed on top of mine behind the sales counter to stop me from wandering off with my friends to skip rope. This foot I knew so well was now paralyzed.

Managing Kent's office, Ma Ma deftly scheduled pushy patients, courageously requested payment, and sternly told patients not to eat in the waiting room. She was in charge. Then without warning, Ma Ma's long streak of soloness spanning decades snapped. The dark brown medicine, thick and pungent, that she had downed faithfully after dinner to control her high blood pressure, had failed. Don't talk about death, she had always warned us, or you will die. She had so carefully avoided the bad omens and courted the good ones, but still she had been brought down. She had wanted a long life, but not like this. Red was for joy, but blue was for grief, a clip of blue yarn in a girl's hair signifying a daughter mourning her mother's death. Never ever do I want to wear blue yarn in my hair. *Dai gut lai see.*

Our fingers bumped as we simultaneously pressed for an "up" elevator. Tomas worked as a marketing manager for a consumer goods company and I was an account manager for an advertising firm. Both companies were located in the same Manhattan skyscraper at the foot of Central Park.

"If you tell me your name, I bet I'll remember it when I see you again," he said. Inside the elevator, he pressed the nineteenth floor and I pressed the thirty-fifth. I had never felt such lift.

He did remember my name, and we went for many

walks, at lunchtime, after work, after dinner. After one walk, as I was waiting to flag a taxi to go home, Tomas lifted his gold chain with an antique Italian coin over his neck and placed it around mine, crowning me like an Olympic gold medalist. Ba Ba would never have done such a thing.

On another walk, we sandwiched in a subway train ride from midtown to Greenwich Village. Tomas somehow kept his balance and mine without gripping the pole or strap. We stood closely in the crowd, chest to chest, rumbling with the ride, magnetized by our matching movements. His breath on my forehead, we did not touch.

On yet another walk, we fantasized about what we would do if we didn't work in a corporation.

"I would want to be a photojournalist, travel and write and take pictures," I said.

That weekend, Tomas presented me with a camera and black-and-white film. "It's better to experiment with black-and-white," he said.

We took my camera on vacation to the Dominican Republic for one week, traveling without reservations and without reservation. We drove in a rental car around the perimeter of the island and then inland, staying in rooms for ten dollars a night at small-town hotels and for one hundred dollars a night at the newest resort with horseback riding on the beach. I took roll after roll of portraits and of hands. With Tomas, I never needed anything more than my passport and my perfume.

"I would want to set up my own import/export trading company, play the stock market, learn to fly, go to law school," Tomas said.

Together we said, "But for now we should open a restaurant."

•   •   •

Ma Ma opens her eyes.

"Look what I brought for you," Tomas says as he puts her hand into the paper bag.

Ma Ma pulls out a cellophane-wrapped pair of Twinkies, her grip denting the sides. This had been a foreign treat that Kent and I were allowed after school every Friday afternoon, and after a while, Ma Ma joined us, somehow finding the soft cake and filling comforting.

"No, thank you," Ma Ma says, pulling her hand away.

"Don't hold his hand," Ma Ma had said, her disapproval fearless. One month before Tomas and I were to be married, we were walking through Chinatown at lunchtime, the bustle of pedestrians and delivery trucks making it as hectic as a pot of boiling minestrone. As a Chinatown child, I had negotiated the confusion of these narrow streets every day. So had the Italian kids from the Catholic school a half block away. They pushed home in groups in their green-and-blue plaid uniforms through Mott and north past Canal Street to Little Italy. It was never a straight line for us from school to home, but a serpentine weave trying to avoid making contact with the Italian kids, as suspenseful as walking through a field of human landmines. What if Ming ran into Joe? What if Tony pushed May? Would we all be late for school after lunch? Would we have to serve detention? Worst of all, would our parents have to meet?

Now the noises were the same, Cantonese whirling past my ears in large sounds of "Where are you going?" and

"Did you eat lunch yet?" The smells were the same, the damp refrigerated truckloads of meat being delivered, the two men bouncing by with a broomstick slung on their shoulders and a slaughtered alabaster pig dangling between them. Even my hunger felt the same, made more unbearable by the fragrances of roast pork and roast duck wafting from open doors of restaurants.

Tomas and I had taken our lunch hour from work uptown and come to meet Ma Ma to go to my bank. Threading through Mott Street as though we were on parade, we were so conspicuous that news of Ma Ma walking with a "white ghost" was buzzing from Chinese mouth to Chinese mouth in rhythm with our footsteps.

"Walk faster. Don't stop. Don't hold his hand," Ma Ma continued in a loud whisper, no, it was a low voice only I heard. She refused to look at anyone—neither me nor any one of her acquaintances gaping at us from the doorsteps of their shops.

I purposely slowed my pace. I slipped my hand out of Tomas's and looped it around his elbow.

"Hurry." Ma Ma hustled us, her steps like daggers and her gaze like a lioness. We were closing the bank account Ma Ma held in trust for me at the Manhattan Savings Bank, the gold-domed building at the foot of the Manhattan Bridge. It was my childhood bank, the one where my twenty dollars a week were deposited by my elementary school, accumulating into a few thousand dollars by college time. Ma Ma was my trustee, and it was hard to tell which brought her more distress, walking down Mott Street with her daughter and future non-Chinese son-in-law, or transferring the money she had seen grow, each quarter and each dollar, one at a time. Had she wasted the money for my orthodontia? What about the money she paid my piano teacher for weekly lessons? Had it all been for naught?

Ma Ma hoped the bank manager, a family friend for over twenty years, would be out to lunch. He wasn't. With a silence between him and Ma Ma like that of two losers in a war, he authorized releasing over eight thousand dollars to me.

But the treaty was still not completed. Ma Ma and I descended further, walking down the flight of stairs at the bank to the safe-deposit vault where the oxygen was stingy and the chrome was filmy. A pressure like underwater submersion came over me.

Ma Ma signed the authorization slip and fingered her copy of the safe-deposit key from her coin purse, a key tied with red bakery-box string for good luck. The clerk looked at Tomas suspiciously, not sure whether he was with us or against us. He could have been a friend, or maybe he was hired to protect us. Surely he was not a *relative*. I nodded a good-bye glance at Tomas as Ma Ma and I carried our box into the small cubicle with a desk and two folding chairs. The room hardly felt private, being ceilingless, but Ma Ma went ahead anyway.

"Why are you doing this?" she asked. She spoke Chinese, as we always did, and no longer in a whisper. Tomas could not understand, but the bank clerk did.

"I would like to take my jewelry," I said. I tried to sound forceful and assured.

Ma Ma was not intimidated. "What will you do with your jewelry?"

By now I was unrolling pieces of gold and jade out of linty facial tissues bound together with thin strips of dried-out rubber bands. The more cherished pieces were zipped in small silk embroidered pouches of red, green, and yellow. Here was a gold necklace with eleven teardrops of jade, five on either side of one large center gem, with matching drop earrings for pierced ears so I wouldn't lose them as I would clip earrings. Here was a thick dragon bangle bracelet in soft, orangey twenty-two-karat gold. Here were seven thin gold bangles in 14K called "day" bracelets, one to add every day of the week. Here were stud earrings of coral in good-luck red with a brooch framed in gold filigree.

The jade and coral and gold spun before my eyes, whirling these colors of a gaudy Chinese restaurant to blur with my tears, tears I could not hold back. I had been so determined to be businesslike doing this, exchanging memories for a future. Tomas and I wanted to sell the jewelry for cash to start our own business. Surely Ma Ma could understand our need to be our own boss, to work for a measure of financial independence. I reached for the old yellowed, crumbling tissue that had all these years wrapped my jewelry, *our* jewelry, these baubles that were symbols of Ma Ma's hard work, to wipe away my tears.

"Tomas and I want to open a restaurant," I managed. "We will sell this for money." Ma Ma noticed I was crying but ignored it. These hard stones and metal in our hands were the tangible results of her years of hard work. She had chalked away money, a ten- or twenty-dollar bill at a time, to make up the hundreds, then thousands, of dollars to buy these items without Ba Ba's knowledge. She didn't know how to buy stocks or how to invest in real estate. That was too complicated and involved anyway, with papers and signatures and even the English language. This she could do on her own. When a friend or a friend's friend arrived new from Hong Kong with jewelry she liked, she bought it, to save for me, for someday. Someday like today.

And now I wanted to change this jewelry back into money.

A small black felt box was tucked in the upper right corner of all these balls of rolled tissue. Ma Ma and I reached for it simultaneously, she knowing what was inside and I having no idea. She let me open it. Tears from a different origin started when I lifted out her engagement ring, a solitaire emerald-cut diamond set in platinum, a ring I recalled seeing on her finger from the time I was doing homework on her lap. How exacting of Ba Ba, to choose a ring so elegant and aesthetically beautiful because of its simplicity. And how rebellious, to choose white and not the garish yellow gold most Chinese prefer. At last, I admired something Ba Ba had done. At last, I saw the beauty of what could have been their marriage.

"Why don't you wear this ring anymore?" I asked.

"It's too dangerous to wear now." She was lying. I slipped the ring on my finger. She could not wear a diamond when there was no longer shine in her marriage. "Anyway, I'm always washing the floor."

"Ma Ma, will you give this ring to me?" I asked. I realized that all this jewelry, the lot of it put together, was less significant to me than this one diamond ring. I needed it to put right Ma Ma and Ba Ba's marriage. I wanted it to bless my own marriage.

"I am saving it for Kent, for his wife when he marries." She took it off my finger and slipped it back into the black box. Case closed.

Tomas and I sold everything except the few pieces which we liked the most. I might someday wear the thick pale jade bangle bracelet or the deep green jade brooch in the shape of a gourd. I haven't yet. Maybe when I am Ma Ma's age.

Chapter Five

ACCUMULATING *FOOK*

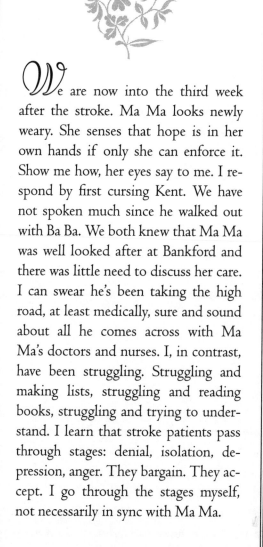

We are now into the third week after the stroke. Ma Ma looks newly weary. She senses that hope is in her own hands if only she can enforce it. Show me how, her eyes say to me. I respond by first cursing Kent. We have not spoken much since he walked out with Ba Ba. We both knew that Ma Ma was well looked after at Bankford and there was little need to discuss her care. I can swear he's been taking the high road, at least medically, sure and sound about all he comes across with Ma Ma's doctors and nurses. I, in contrast, have been struggling. Struggling and making lists, struggling and reading books, struggling and trying to understand. I learn that stroke patients pass through stages: denial, isolation, depression, anger. They bargain. They accept. I go through the stages myself, not necessarily in sync with Ma Ma.

"The major effect of your mother's stroke is that she has hemiplegia," her doctor explains to me when he stops by during his rounds. "That's paralysis on one side of the body. A stroke in the right side of the brain affects the left side, as in your mother's case, and vice versa.

"Everything else will subside with time, her swelling, her drooling, her swallowing difficulties," he continues. "Most of all, her mental capacity seems almost totally intact. And she does not have any vision or speech impairment. She doesn't have aphasia, where she can't express herself or understand others, and she doesn't have agnosia, where she doesn't know what certain things are for and who certain people are, as many stroke patients do. You should really think about where your mother goes from here. . . ."

Yes, yes, but, her paralysis . . . Can you undo that?

There is no answer, and the doctor leaves.

Ma Ma remains trapped in her bed. She understands nothing of what her doctor has just said to me. She slowly turns, lying on her immobile left side, and lets slip a "Jenny, my daughter, heart of my heart" out of the corner of her mouth.

My eyes become unfocused and my tears burn their way upward through my heart.

Ma Ma pulls herself more upright in bed, her left jaw regaining some of her rigidness, her spine stiffening.

Don't lose to anything, she says. Don't let them see you beaten. Besides, crying will ruin your eyes. Remember the Other Jenny, she says.

Ma Ma had breast-fed the Other Jenny a day after I was born. A new nurse had brought the Other Jenny to her, and Ma Ma noticed the difference at once. This baby was suckling at her breast too indelicately. This cannot be my daughter, Ma Ma said to herself. The Other Jenny was in fact her roommate's baby, a baby whose father would die of tuberculosis only three years later. Her mother, a Chinese woman who lived on Bayard Street, spent years crying for her dead husband until she went blind.

"*Ai ya, say la!*" the Other Jenny's mother rumbled the streets she walked, death in her every stomp. "Let me die!" She was a constant, moaning figure on Bayard.

"*Ai ya,*" Ma Ma said. "Imagine losing your husband and losing your eyesight as well!"

I avoided like a witch the Other Jenny whose birthday was the day after mine, who grew up around the corner, who sat behind me in class, and who shared my name. This Other Jenny, her mother and her siblings never seemed quite as fortunate as my family. Our clothes and shoes were newer. We ate leaner cuts of meat and fresh fish. Our apartment was larger than theirs and had its own bathroom. Kent and I did better at school. Ma Ma used that family to explain the forces that come together to form one's destiny, one's *fook* or happiness, which is represented by a Chinese character composed of four smaller characters: a roof to symbolize shelter; a field to promise plenty of food; a mouth for good health; and clothes for warmth. You need all four to have happiness. But obviously there's more to it than that. The Other Jenny's family had all four and they were not happy, were they? Ma Ma explained that living a Chinese life, you had to accumulate *fook* as you lived. Never, never, for example, click chopsticks together when sitting down to a meal. Or tap them on the table like drumsticks. That would be an omen for a fight and bring bad luck. Never, ever stick chopsticks upright in a bowl of rice, for that would be disrespectful, too much like incense sticks used for worshipping dead ancestors. Propping your chin on one hand while eating with the other is less mannerly than elbows on the table. How can you be so gloomy when there is food on your table? Fearing the Other Jenny's lack of *fook*, I never completely emptied out the container for storing rice because I feared having no more, suffering the famine that Ma Ma and her family faced during the war. To this day, I hold myself back from using beautiful and sleek white candles with my silver candlesticks because white is the Chinese color of mourning, brides wearing white and red. This *fook* can be passed along, Ma Ma said, like a trust fund, and those who suffer most, accumulate the most *fook*. And she has been very busy saving a lifetime for us.

Don't cry, Jenny, don't ruin your *fook*, Ma Ma says to me. I hear but I do not feel. I want Ma Ma, the way she used to be. I don't want to be the educated consumer anymore, listening to doctors say "hemiplegia" and "aphasia." I don't want to think. I only want to *feel*. If only I can distinguish where Ma Ma's *fook* ends and mine begins.

I reach down and take off my shoes. I grope for the privacy curtain, transforming the hospital bed into a canopied crib, and crawl into bed, climbing over the rail, to Ma Ma. I push and roll her over a little with my knees to make a space for me to lie down next to her, head to head, shoulder to shoulder, hand to hand. For a few moments I am a little girl again on Saturday mornings, the one morning each week when there was neither a rush to school nor to church nor to open the store. Ma Ma would be in her bed alone those mornings, Ba Ba sleeping in a separate room, their marriage already in disrepair. She would pull the covers back, a scratchy, colorful Southwestern serape from her cousin in Tucson, folding a V-shaped piece of blanket over herself with her left hand and stretching out her right arm into a crescent onto which my head fell. Sometimes I would lie with the nape of my neck in the crook of her arm, eyes closed, face up toward the ceiling. Or I would nestle my ear inside her elbow, inhaling Ma Ma's morning scent deeply. I felt the smoothness of her skin still taut but lacking the elasticity of youth, the warmth and softness of her inner thighs with my cold feet, the roughness of the callouses on her hands that snagged strands of my long hair.

Lying in the hospital bed, Ma Ma feels incomprehensibly strong holding me. I smooth her hair and lift her awkward, motionless left arm to adjust the blanket around her midriff. I cradle her head in my arm. Ma Ma is broken in body but not in spirit. I can feel it now.

"Don't cry, Jenny," she repeats. Ma Ma has not been defeated. I know at that moment that I have a winner on my hands.

I am not so sure about the rest of us.

Chapter Six

SO STUPID

$\mathcal{I}$ call my brother. "Kent, I'm at Bankford and the doctor just asked me about Ma Ma's plans after discharge. Can I stop by? Have you had dinner yet?"

"No, I just got home," Kent says, missing not a beat. We always pick up in midsentence, no matter what the sentiment. "Come on up. I'll order some sushi."

That was the way with Kent. I am always his little sister.

I remember the bully's face was round, his hands pudgy, and his hair a flat-top crew cut. I remember his name to be Johnny, but Kent swears his name was Jimmy. He was in sixth grade, two years older than me. Every day at the heavy black enamel front gates of school at dismissal time, he looked at all of me, a skinny nine-year-old girl, through narrow eyes. Then one day he was running past me, giving my right braid behind my back a tug so strong my nose hit the sky and tears fell to my earlobes. He did this for a week, maybe two. It was because he liked me, Kent said, which made the tugging even more repulsive.

"Run, Jenny, run!" my friend May crouched and hollered.

I ran, but the pulling and running clung on like dead bugs on a car grille. Until one afternoon Kent waited in a dark doorway two buildings from the school. When Johnny or Jimmy the bully ran past with his sights on me, Kent rounded his right leg out and planted the bottom of his shoe so firmly in J's behind that his feet skimmed the ground for a few steps like a hydrofoil. After that my running stopped and my pigtails were left alone.

Even now it doesn't matter whether Kent is fishing in Belize or I am sailing in the British Virgin Islands. We are always somehow connected by Johnny or Jimmy the bully and the bumpy stroller ride to City Hall. Kent always knows the right thing to do.

When I arrive at Kent's, he is still in his green surgical scrubs but is already taking the sushi, piece by piece, out of the Styrofoam boxes and placing each rectangle of raw fish and rice onto black-and-white-specked plates of puffy ceramic.

"It's okay, don't bother. I'll eat it out of the box," I say. I was so used to my kids.

"Yeah, but it tastes better this way." He laughs. Kent has somehow along the way acquired a professorial air, his hair at the temples a brush of white and his Italian shoes sleek but comfortable.

He turns and opens his freezer and clinks ice cubes into crystal highball tumblers with a teardrop bubble in the thick base. Our drinking containers of choice at home were a set of plastic Ninja Turtle cups in purple, red, orange, and blue. Kent offers me some strawberry wine cooler, probably the newest brand, that he bought from the Korean deli at the corner. He was always on the edge, up on the latest of trends. Does Kent even have designer chopsticks? I thought. We sit in what will be the dining room postrenovation, at an old worktable covered by a crisp cotton sheet facing the almost-done kitchen. I haven't felt so New York reverse chic since . . . since before.

Oh, we were all so busy with our lives. I watch him as he dips his sushi into low-sodium soy sauce and places the whole piece in his mouth. My big brother suddenly seems small, the bite of sushi oversized for his mouth, and he becomes a solemn boy concerned about his mother, agonized by a measure of guilt.

I dab and swirl some wasabi mustard into my soy sauce and place a sliver of pink preserved ginger on my tongue. I look around his apartment and wonder what woman will someday slip into his life and share this with him. He has always had one girlfriend or another, some of whom I even tried to matchmake with him.

"I've been worrying about Ma Ma," I say. "The doctor asked me again tonight what our plans are. I want her to come home with me. To live with us."

"You can't do that, Jenny," Kent says as he plops a sea urchin *uni* sushi into his mouth. To him, it tasted like peanut butter of the sea. To me, it tasted like the bottom of the ocean. I always gave mine to him. "You've got your kids to worry about."

"So she'll be like my fourth kid. . . ."

"I don't think so. It's not that simple." Kent finishes

half his sushi and starts to dig in the bag for his box of cold buckwheat noodles. He slides the noodles out onto a clean plate and carefully drizzles the sauce equally around. His motions are familiar: the same lucid wrist as Ba Ba drizzling peanut oil on Ma Ma's vegetables.

"What do you know about it? You don't have kids yet." I start to clear the table of empty boxes, stacking the plastic soy sauce containers, dabbing the tablecloth with the soft white paper napkins. I am Supermom, don't you see? Miss Efficient. Trying to impress Kent. Or convince myself.

"Hey, I'm not finished with that yet." Kent grabs one of the boxes to eat the long thin shreds of turnip garnish. I continue to organize and to clean, feeling my breath get short, the same frenzy I feel when Tomas and I argued. All of a sudden, I become a television commercial whiz mom for cleaning products, my words coming out as forcefully as I am scrubbing.

"Look, I'll dress her, I'll cook for her, I'll take her to the park . . . I can manage it."

"But there's more to it than that. You've got to see the whole picture, Jen."

"What else is there? She's my mother!"

"She's my mother too!"

Yes, but I'd seen how he had acted after Ma Ma's stroke—he could not control her.

"I told you to stop fussing with the garbage that night," Kent had said weakly. "You should have stopped. . . . Why didn't you stop?"

"I know, it's my fault," Ma Ma had tried to say, a guilt in her voice, too. "*Ai!* I deserve it!"

Kent goes back to eating his sushi. "Look, Jen, Ma Ma

won't be able to handle *your* kids well. I know. Some old folk are like that."

I feel my throat wrap around the sliver of ginger I've been sucking. I stop cleaning, fussing with the boxes. "That's precisely it. I don't want her in some old folk's home. Ma Ma's been alone all her life. She'll be all alone there. She never had Ba Ba. She has only us."

I push my chair back, being careful not to scratch the antiqued pine floor, and start to wash the plates. The running water is soothing and drowning, to my ears and to my hands. "I've got to take care of her. Please, let me take care of her."

"Here, let me do that," Kent says, trying to take the plate from my hand.

"I'll teach her. I'll show her . . ." I would not let go of the plate. It was war. Who can wash the plate better?

"You just don't get it." Kent is too calm. "Ma Ma's got to learn to take care of herself. There's a great rehabilitation program at Randal Institute."

"Damn it, Kent, you think you have it all figured out! You just don't understand. You're just like Tomas. You want everybody else to do everything. I'm not sending her away. She belongs with me."

"She'll only end up feeling like a burden." Kent's volume is all of a sudden up a few notches. "I should know. I've seen patients who don't even want help walking into my exam room. They want to be on their own. They hate it when they can't."

A burden. With a tight feeling in my chest, I realize that that's exactly what Ma Ma has been. A burden. But I don't want to resent it. I can't resent it. I am a good Chinese daughter, my mother's daughter.

I gulp down my last piece of sushi over the sink, a good Chinese daughter cannot waste any food. "Here, you do it!" I shove the plate into his hands. "I'm out of it! I'm going home."

I slam the door behind me, and I hear the echoing hollow of his semirenovated loft through the metal door. Good. Let him suffer for a change.

Arriving home, I walk through our front door and immediately hear the low family roar. A teenager with nonstop phone calls and parties, a four-year-old banging on an electronic keyboard, and a one-year-old crawling around table legs and learning to walk. The noise is sweet to my ears; who wouldn't relish it?

So why am I struggling not to cry?

Damn it. And damn it some more.

I pick up the phone.

"So, where is the Randal Institute?" I ask.

"It's part of a university, on Thirty-fourth Street." Kent is always in sync.

"But it will be just temporary, right? Until Ma Ma gets back on her feet."

We both laugh at my slip. "We'll see, Jen. Let's see how it goes."

"So Ma Ma will come live with me after Randal. Randal . . . isn't it near Macy's?" I fasten on one of our inside jokes. "Hey, remember 'So Stupid'?"

"So stu-u-u-pid!" Kent and I are laughing together again.

It didn't used to be funny. Not when Ba Ba spewed it at Ma Ma, at almost anyone, as a refrain. He chastised all the little idiots for being so inferior to him, especially Ma Ma.

He rewrote the price labels for the items in the gift shop that Ma Ma had written because he didn't like her handwriting. "So stupid!" It was one of his few contributions to the shop.

He made her wash the shop window twice because to his eyes the first time was not clean enough. "So stupid!"

He returned shoes Ma Ma bought for us because he was sure he could buy shoes with more supportive arches. "So stupid!"

In time almost everyone in Ba Ba's path was stupid in one way or another, even the Macy's shoe salesman.

"Give me shoes like this for her," he said, pointing at my twelve-year-old feet with one hand and holding what had to be a square-toed brown orthopedic shoe in the other. How I had yearned for pointy-toed black patent leather shoes instead.

The salesman asked what size I wore.

"Size five," I answered.

Ba Ba yanked my hand to shut my mouth. He asked the salesman to measure my feet.

"It's not necessary," the salesman said. How unsuspecting of him.

"Then how do you know what size she wears?" Ba Ba challenged.

"She wears size five. I'll bring a size five and a size six. . . ."

Ba Ba was appalled to be buying shoes by trial and error. A quick measure by the standard metal fitter plate would have determined my exact size, and that should be the size I wore regardless of the fit or the last or the brand name.

"Not necessary?! Not necessary?! So stupid! *You* not necessary!" Ba Ba yanked my hand again and left without buying shoes of any size.

So stupid! So were Mr. and Mrs. Silverman, regular customers of Ma Ma's who had an Upper East Side apartment filled with Chinese knickknacks from decades of travel. They became fond of Ma Ma and watched Kent and me grow from toddlers to schoolchildren, but they always left our shop whenever Ba Ba entered. The Christmas after I started kindergarten, Mr. and Mrs. Silverman came to the shop not to buy but to give—a silvery gun in a brown holster for Kent and a tan cowgirl hat with matching tassled skirt for me.

"Where did you get these?" Ba Ba demanded when he discovered our treasured presents.

"The Silvermans," we said, "the Silvermans gave them to us for Christmas."

"No, we don't accept gifts from customers," Ba Ba said.

"But, why? They're our friends."

"No, they are not friends. You give them back." Ba Ba's voice escalated and his jaw clenched. The vein in his temple began to pound.

"But we want them, we like them!"

"No!" He grabbed them from us, then turned to Ma Ma, and said, "So stupid! We don't know anything about them. Don't you know they could be with the CIA? The FBI? The IRS? They could report us!"

Ma Ma didn't understand all these letters nor anything about us the Silvermans could report, but a toy gun and a cowgirl hat were not worth such disharmony. She took our gifts from us and hid them under the counter, returning them to the Silvermans on their next shopping trip.

So stupid! So was Ba Ba's army buddy, Mr. Lai.

Already half past eleven and already another August scorcher, it was too hot and too humid to hang around Chinatown again. Mr. Lai had been waiting for almost two hours, the third time in the past two weeks, but Ba Ba was just having his breakfast of one egg, toast, and coffee, in that precise order, preferring first the soft-boiled egg scooped out into a small cup, then the toast cut into quarters, and finally the coffee dark as can be with only a drop or two of milk. His egg was best bordering on four minutes when the yolk was the same orange ball as a sunset into a cloudy horizon after a summer rain, and his toast had to be just so, lightly browned and lightly buttered. No one else could do it exactly to his liking. These noises of Ba Ba, the cracking of the eggshell, the scraping of the toast, and the rustling fold of newspapers, linger in caverns of my memory where the familiar sounds of feet walking through autumn leaves and ringing bells of ice cream trucks are stored.

"Go see what your father is doing," Mr. Lai ordered us from the front steps after too much time had passed. Our skin was sporting a layer of moisture just from standing around.

"We don't have to go. We know he just got up and he's eating breakfast," Kent and I said together, backing each other up.

"But he said to come at nine-thirty to go swimming at Coney Island. It's already lunchtime." Mr. Lai paused, wondering whether he should go on. "There will be so many people at Washington Pool, there won't be any lockers left."

We were convinced and we ran into the apartment to

check on Ba Ba. "Come on, Ba Ba, let's go! Mr. Lai is waiting. The pool will be too crowded."

"Tell Mr. Lai not to rush me." Ba Ba's jaw began to
come down hard on his toast.

But we had courage backed by Mr. Lai. "He's all
packed and he's been waiting," we said.

"Let him wait. I will be ready."

"He said he'll go without us. . . ."

"So stupid!" Ba Ba threw down his toast. "Then tell
Mr. Lai to go to hell!"

Kent and I don't know whether Mr. Lai did or did
not. We only know we did not go to Coney Island on that
day. Or for many days thereafter.

So stupid. Not necessary.

And that's how I feel as my conversation with Kent ends.

Chapter Seven

SPILLED RICE

$\mathcal{M}$a Ma is having her first vacation in forty years. Because of her age, no one is very pushy about getting her up and moving to keep the nerves and muscles damaged from the stroke from rigidifying and atrophying. She is actually waiting for a bed at the Randal Institute, but we keep the joke alive that her gaggle of wires are crossed, a common Chinese insult, and we are waiting for the telephone man to come and reconnect them.

Even after all the arrangements and paperwork have been made and we have discussed the upcoming move several times with Ma Ma, she still does not understand. "Why can't I go home if I'm fine now?" she asks again as I roll her pajamas neatly into the duffel bag. I am tired of being the only one who can pack perfectly. I am tired of explaining rehabilitation therapy, for which words in Chinese I do not even know. I am tired of feeling guilty, mad at Kent for putting me in this position.

"You have to go to Randal for rehabilitation therapy."

"What is that? What is habitation rappy?"

"*Re*habilitation ther—" I begin, then give up. I was never able to explain osteoporosis or estrogen replacement therapy to her either. "They will teach you to walk with a cane. They will teach you how to get dressed. They will teach you how to eat by yourself." All things I could have taught her. If Kent had not insisted. If I had not listened to Kent. If I had been a better daughter.

Ma Ma looks at me like a fresh fish with bulging eyes at the market. She has been tolerating all this nonsense at the hospital so that she can go home. Now we are telling her she is heading to yet another foreign place with foreign foods, training for yet another mission like an astronaut.

The light spring rain today hurries me, and I try to transfer Ma Ma from under Bankford's canopy to the van quickly. The umbrella becomes a struggle and a weapon. Ma Ma never liked getting her hair wet—"It will give you headaches when you are old," she had warned me whenever I went to school with damp hair. I can feel Ma Ma's own hurry, her impatience trying to rev the wheelchair. Still, the rain is good luck, good *feng-shui*, like rain on a Chinese bride on her wedding day, rain that washes her and her family to come with harmony.

Ma Ma is carsick on the half-hour ride from Bankford to Randal and sucking on salty Chinese dried plums barely helps. She keeps quiet, except for the rustling cellophane package in her lap, hoping that keeping words down will keep down her nausea. But when I wheel her through the glass doors into Randal, she says, "You're pushing me too fast."

First too slow, now too fast. I have to resist the urge to push her even faster.

In the elevator, I stare at her right hand, the hundred caulk-white lines, the veins like blue worms, the knuckles almost skinless as she grips the armrest of her wheelchair. This hand is my hand.

We travel twelve floors to Ma Ma's new room, actually a ward, facing the East River. She becomes quiet and listless again as I settle her into her area, busying myself the way I would in a new hotel room, checking the light switches, turning on the sink faucet and the TV, opening the window. The choppers at the heliport by the river are struggling in the rain and wind. Ma Ma concentrates on adjusting to the new height of her room, having lived on the ground floor in Chinatown, then on the fifth at Bankford. She is moving up. Soon she will get new food to complain about.

Ma Ma's ward is like a large dormitory suite. She has three "roommates." I introduce everyone. It feels like the first day of school. One roommate, a man in his twenties named Mike, has injured his upper spine in a motorcycle accident. He has a steel rod in his back, he says with something like pride, and both of his arms and legs are paralyzed. His neck is wrapped in a stiff, thick white brace. I can see Ma Ma quickly calculating. At least she has the use of one good arm and one good leg. Another roommate, younger than Mike, has caught a bullet in his spine. Herman was once commander of his neighborhood, king of his sidewalks, but now he has two unusable legs. His arms and shoulders are muscular, and I can tell he would be a marvel at wheelchair basketball. Ma Ma's third roommate is a woman in her early fifties who has also had a stroke, a brain attack in her left brain that affected the right side of her body, her speech and memory. She seems to be in a daze, not really understanding what is being said to her. Ma Ma thinks: Look, she's much younger than me and at least I can speak more clearly. How lucky I am. *Dai gut lai see.*

On our tour of the therapy room, Ma Ma is in awe of all the metal contraptions and paraphernalia that are outfitted for the patients. Her "therapist manager" is Jane Dorsey, a compact woman with a high-volume voice and strong glasses and brown curly hair that she pulls back with a banana comb.

"Your mom's going to be okay," Jane Dorsey says as she shakes my hand. How would *she* know whether Ma Ma was going to be okay? She's just seen Ma Ma for a few minutes; I've been with her for the past few months. Already Jane Dorsey is taking over.

But Jane Dorsey does not put out her hand to shake Ma Ma's. She knows to wait, and when Ma Ma raises her right hand like a salute, Jane Dorsey grabs it like a high five. The camaraderie is instantaneous between them, and I feel like the Macy's shoe salesman.

Ma Ma keeps smiling, thinking like a kindergartner that "making nice" will help her make friends. "Jane is very nice," she says, still holding her hand. "And so strong."

Gosh, I just walked into a mutual admiration society.

"What kind of regimen will you put my mother on?" I ask.

"We'll begin by trying to strengthen her hand and arm muscles, both her left side and right, with something like this," Jane Dorsey says as she pulls out a dull red egg with finger loops, what looks like rubber brass knuckles, from the pocket of her white cotton pants. How handy. Just like the guitarist who always carries a pick or the horse lover who hides a lump of sugar. "Squeezing this is harder than it looks, but it will make your mother concentrate on building her strength. She'll feel like she's accomplishing something. She can just keep it in her hand and squeeze it all day long."

In spite of Jane Dorsey, I am off on my own fantasy: Ma Ma once again is able to grip a rice bowl in one hand and chopsticks in the other. She can shell a long, crumbly peanut shaped like a woman. She can hold up a compact, look into its mirror, and draw on her rose lipstick. But Jane Dorsey interrupts me, and I find my hand intercepting the rubber egg she is trying to put into Ma Ma's left hand. The egg feels surprisingly heavy and hard. Jane Dorsey vacates my hand, gives the egg to Ma Ma, and says, "Squeeze, Mrs. Liang . . . that's right." Look at the two of them, exchanging toys already. "Try to *feel* the muscles." The strain in Ma Ma's left wrist is obvious, the tendons hardly able to pull.

Jane Dorsey then leads us to a walking platform, a ten-foot-long wooden plank with handrails on each side, sort of a double-sided ballet barre. "Some of your mother's muscles were more damaged by the stroke than others. So now she has to substitute, you know, use muscles that were least affected," she explains. "I'll certainly put your mother through her paces here, won't I!" she says with a laugh and a glance to me. The enthusiasm can be eaten with a spoon, and I've already stopped translating for Ma Ma. But Ma Ma takes the laughter for fun. Little does she know.

"Ma Ma's never been to a gym before," I say. "She's going to find this difficult. . . ."

"That's no problem. She'll learn fast. Right, Mrs. Liang?" This time she smiles at Ma Ma and adjusts the banana comb in her hair.

"Yes, yes, Jane Dorsey," Ma Ma replies.

We move on to the Steps to Nowhere—four wooden steps with rubber strips inlaid on each step, again with handrails on each side. "Up with the good and down with the bad," Jane Dorsey chants as she demonstrates. I wonder whether it would be easier to back down the steps, like Anni crawling backward down the stairs. Ma Ma hears the others working on the exercise machines, the clanking tower of metal weights one atop the other, but to her, it is more like the clacking brown wooden abacus beads. I'd like to see Jane Dorsey get Ma Ma into spandex.

I breathe down Jane Dorsey's neck as she begins to keep Ma Ma's exercise log book as neatly as I have been keeping my children's baby books. Jane Dorsey moves forward a step as she continues writing. "I'm responsible for determining how much your mother can actually do," she answers without my question. "I factor in her age, her physical condition before the stroke, the severity of the stroke itself. I like to push the limit a little to challenge her, but I don't want to frustrate her."

"What about everyday activities?" I ask. "Like dressing and eating?"

"Oh, I'll be teaching self-dressing," Jane Dorsey says, "and Mrs. Sampson will teach eating. In fact, it's lunchtime now."

We return to Ma Ma's room just as Mrs. Sampson brings in everyone's lunch on green plastic trays and stays to feed Ma Ma, the new pupil, who does not even flinch when Mrs. Sampson swings a thin plastic bib over her head and ties it behind her neck. If only Mrs. Sampson had been with us at Bankford during our gelatin days.

This mealtime is more like classtime with Mrs. Sampson the sommelier teaching the appreciation of self-supported eating. The class moves on after soup drinking that soils all the bibs, and Mrs. Sampson hands everyone forks with the same bent neck as the spoons. I can see in Ma Ma that these crooked utensils with curves pointing the ladle and tongs toward the mouth will never replace chopsticks, just as mashed potatoes will never substitute for rice. A plate of food divided into three sections will never satisfy like a bowl of rice and an entrée at table center for everyone to share. Ma Ma manages through the pasta, today served with marinara sauce, without seeming too much to be playing with her food, but she does not use her napkin even once. Her lips are translucent orange and particularly oily around the edges, and her bib and chin sport a few assorted tomato spots as well.

On another afternoon visit, I walk in on a dressing lesson.

"See, you put your left arm into the sleeve first," Jane Dorsey is saying. "That's right. Then you pull your left arm through the armhole with your right arm. Slip your right arm through." Ma Ma's left arm and hand are never referred to as her "bad" arm and hand.

Ma Ma is putting on the bright red T-shirt, size XL, that I just bought for her a few days earlier from the Gap, alongside clothes for Anni from Baby Gap next door. I had been wandering through the store in a fashion twilight zone when a sudden advertising vision came to me: Ma

Ma and Anni as beautiful models for a Gap ad in a moody, grainy black-and-white photo taken by high-fashion photographer Steven Meisel. They are wearing white T-shirts and gray sweats, Ma Ma sitting in her wheelchair with her aging chubbiness and Anni in her stroller with her baby fat. "Style you never outgrow," the caption would read.

"Now, this sweatshirt is great because it's open in the front." Jane Dorsey gives me an approving look for having bought it. "Let your right hand pull your left arm through the sleeve, just like the T-shirt." She helps Ma Ma maneuver her arms through, and surprisingly, Ma Ma's left arm is stubborn and tight at the elbow. "That's normal," says Jane Dorsey. "It's called spasticity. Easy, now.

"Okay, with the pants, it's also one at a time. You put the left leg in first, pull it as far as you can under your seat. Then put your right leg in and up to your waist. There." Jane Dorsey makes the movements crisp and clean, a modern dance choreographer, and Ma Ma follows along, lagging some.

Although it is Jane Dorsey who prescribes the regimen for Ma Ma, it is Tony who becomes Ma Ma's right arm—and leg. He is Puerto Rican, he says, but was born in New York City. To me, he is very *West Side Story*. Maybe Ma Ma sees the romance in it too. I have never seen her take to a "white ghost" the way she does Tony, holding his hand longer than necessary.

Previously Ma Ma's idea of exercise was sitting in the shade under a parasol. Only peasants had muscles from spending hours on end in the fields. Only peasants sweated in the rice paddies. Ladies of class embroidered silk or painted watercolors or played the *pi pa* indoors, their skin translucent and sweat free. Now Ma Ma in her seventh decade is redefining herself, huffing and puffing with Tony.

"Look at these muscles!" Tony says with a squeeze of Ma Ma's shoulders and biceps with each word. Ma Ma giggles at the tickle. "We have to make them even stronger, don't we?" Then Tony turns to me, and says, "We have to work on her right side so she can support her weak side. For when she does everything. Getting in her wheelchair. Getting out. Getting in and out of bed, going to the bathroom."

Tony puts a two-pound weight in Ma Ma's right hand. With her forearm resting on the arm of her wheelchair, he helps her curl five sets of ten, spotting her like a mother bird.

"*Uno, dos, tres, quatro . . .*" he counts in Spanish.

"*Yut, yee, som, say . . .*" Ma Ma repeats in Chinese.

Then they reverse, Tony counting in Chinese, Ma Ma in Spanish. They've been teaching each other.

Tony continues the exercises by raising Ma Ma's elbow out to her shoulder height and curling her arm in. Five sets of ten again. Finally, what is most difficult of all, Tony raises Ma Ma's arm straight over her head. She is afraid the weight will drop on her head and shrinks into her shoulder. Tony now giggles at her nervous laugh. He places one hand over her head to reassure her that it will not fall and helps her move the weight up and down, practically caressing her.

Now, a couple of weeks into Randal, Ma Ma does not make a move without Tony. They've become quite a pair.

"Tony, Tony!" I hear Ma Ma say when I arrive one morning. "Please, toilet." Thank goodness his name is not

Stanislav or Lorenzo. Tony comes swiftly from across the room to her left side and leans over the arm of her wheelchair. He seems the perfect height, neither too tall nor too short, an inch or so taller than I am. I guess five foot eight. He hooks his bronze right forearm under Ma Ma's left shoulder.

"Lean against me. Yes, like this," he says, pulling her weight against his inside chest. It is a strange intimacy for me to witness, Ma Ma in such close physical contact with a man. Then Tony stretches his right arm across Ma Ma's breasts and clasps his right hand with Ma Ma's right hand. He closes his left hand with hers and lifts her in one move to standing position, as smoothly as an Olympic contender pressing two hundred and fifty pounds overhead in one clean jerk.

Ma Ma is very, very wobbly in standing position, so much heavier on her immobilized left side and so much weaker. Together with Tony, the two of them are a body and a half, and they move like synchronized swimmers. As Tony begins to shuffle Ma Ma toward the toilet, I can see the damage that the stroke has imposed on her. She moves choppily, like a flip-book cartoon character with some pages missing.

Ma Ma's face shows a concentration and determination she musters up from someplace within, where *chi*, that elusive essential energy, comes from. With their backs to the toilet, Tony motions that Ma Ma can lower her pants with her good right hand.

"Don't worry. I won't let you fall," Tony says. But that is hardly what is worrying her. Not wanting Tony to become impatient with her, Ma Ma leans over a bit and bunches down her pants from her waist to her thigh with her right hand. She pulls, and her pants slide down on an angle, caught on her left hip. She pulls some more, and down they fall. Then her underpants. Tony lowers her into the seat, steps outside and closes the door.

So just in the last fifteen minutes, Ma Ma has held hands with a man, had her breasts brushed by him, and lowered her pants in his presence. All without a hint of modesty, or a word of complaint. She is exhausted when she makes the round trip from the bathroom that lands her again in her wheelchair. Her forehead is clammy, her breath in rapid short takes, the physical effect comparable to my running five miles. At this rate it must take all her energy just to get to the bathroom and back a few times a day.

Who *was* this woman, this woman with orange lips and fingers entwined in Tony's? Was this *my* Ma Ma who had warmed my spot in bed with her body on winter nights when I was a child and who set aside enough money for my airfare to Taiwan for a cultural exchange program when I was a teenager? Was she the mother who could not divorce because to divorce would be to break up the Chinese character for "good," with the symbol for "girl" on the left and for "boy" on the right, by leaving Kent with Ba Ba and taking me away? This was my Ma Ma who survived her marriage by repeating to herself day after day: Sacrifice. Sacrifice. Sacrifice. Life was not silk and cashmere but a chain of our own misery so others can be happy. There was cause and effect, don't you see? Her misery produced our happiness.

And now her stroke was her greatest sacrifice yet.

I have to get away.

"I must go now, Ma Ma," I say abruptly.

Ma Ma turns her attention to me. "Don't leave. Watch me."

"No, I can't. I have to go home. I have to cook dinner."

I kiss her good-bye.

"Good-bye, my dearest daughter. Eat a lot. Eat more. You're too skinny."

The crowd says good-bye, each in turn, and I give them a collective wave.

At home, I race to get dinner on the table, against whom or what I don't know.

"Mark, stop throwing that ball around. I'm cooking now," I say over the kitchen counter. He continues to toss the orange sponge football made for indoor passing around the dining table. He's a one-man team, the quarterback and the wide receiver.

I try a different tack: "Mark, how about giving the remote control car a whirl?"

It doesn't work. I'm at such a loss, myself a missile without a known trajectory, and the ball comes spiraling over the open counter into the kitchen, a touchdown at the lidless rice canister. The sound is like heavy Brazilian rain as tens of thousands of ivory kernels scatter on the tiles.

"Look what you've done!" I am shaking now. "Why can't you listen to me and do as I say?"

Mark races to my side, crouching next to my bent knees. He cradles his ball under his arm and cups one hand. With the other hand, he tries to pick up the rice, one by one, but his little fingers are too huge for the kernels.

I grasp his wrist, stopping him, and start to push the rice together into a pile to scoop with my own cupped hands. Mark sees that I am crying, crying over spilled rice, rice that I cannot control.

"Do you know how unlucky this is?" I say. "If Grand Ma Ma saw this, she would—"

"I'm sorry, Mommy. I'm sorry to Grand Ma Ma, too." Mark starts to gather his own pile.

I put our piles together and scoop the mountain into the pot. Not into the garbage. I turn on the water and start to rinse the rice, swirling my hand into the off-white scum.

"Mommy, we're going to eat this rice?" Mark is in disbelief.

"Yes, of course, why not?"

"Eeewwww!!! That's dirty. I'm not going to eat it."

"Yes, you are. We're all going to eat it. We never waste rice."

That night, for our bedtime reading, I pull out a well-worn and well-read chunky square book, *Ernie Gets Dressed,* for Anni. Mark joins us for the snuggle. There are tabs on the right of the book with a picture of each piece of clothing Ernie layers on: undershirt, underpants, T-shirt, pants, sweater, socks, shoes, coat, hat. On each page a simple sentence describes the action.

"Ernie puts on a T-shirt," I read as Anni turns the tabbed page. "Just like Anni . . ."

"Ernie puts on pants," I read. "Like Anni does . . ."

"Ernie wears shoes," I read. "Shoes like Anni's . . ."

Yes, and Grand Ma Ma's. Perhaps I should bring this book to Randal. My mental *lop sop* is becoming a clawing monster. I cannot shake it even at night with Tomas. Ma Ma looms large in our bed, and nothing is the same: Tomas's touch, his breathing, his scent, his space where I lovingly roam, mine where Ma Ma seems to haunt.

"Come closer," Tomas says, wrapping his arms even tighter around me. I am feeling small, as though he can encircle me at least twice and then some. And I am feeling thin, as though he can breathe the vapor that is me and I will disappear. Tomas pulls me toward him, and a force I have never felt pulls me the other way.

"Why, why can't I let go?" I say, speaking to the ceiling.

"Jenny, you're not responsible for everything and everybody. You don't have to be a female Atlas, you know." Tomas sounds angry and impatient.

"I feel so helpless, so out of control," I say, as though not hearing him.

"Ma Ma's not like an advertising account you might lose," Tomas says. "You might lose something else," he adds, turning away.

Chapter Eight

CHINESE SONS

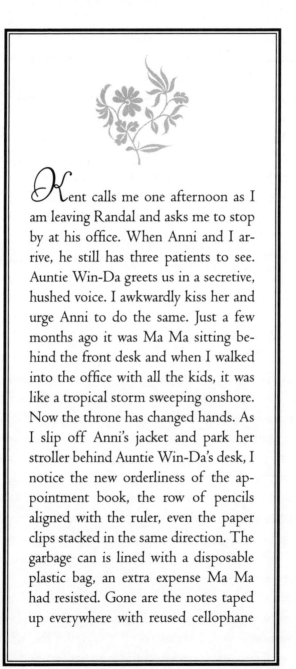

$\mathcal{K}$ent calls me one afternoon as I am leaving Randal and asks me to stop by at his office. When Anni and I arrive, he still has three patients to see. Auntie Win-Da greets us in a secretive, hushed voice. I awkwardly kiss her and urge Anni to do the same. Just a few months ago it was Ma Ma sitting behind the front desk and when I walked into the office with all the kids, it was like a tropical storm sweeping onshore. Now the throne has changed hands. As I slip off Anni's jacket and park her stroller behind Auntie Win-Da's desk, I notice the new orderliness of the appointment book, the row of pencils aligned with the ruler, even the paper clips stacked in the same direction. The garbage can is lined with a disposable plastic bag, an extra expense Ma Ma had resisted. Gone are the notes taped up everywhere with reused cellophane tape; in their place a few yellow Post-it squares. The appointment book is legibly written, the names neatly contained within each line. I keep my eye on Auntie Win-Da and see her technique: she uses a ruler to guide her script, like a child.

Auntie Win-Da is not really my aunt, that is, she is not Ma Ma's blood sister. But perhaps more important she is Ma Ma's *jeah jeah*, her big sister, an upperclassman from their school days together at the Pui Jing School for Girls in Canton, China, in the 1930s. "Auntie" is how we Chinese children address our parents' closest friends. Auntie Win-Da may not have been a relative, but in my child's eye she was one better. She was an empress, a royal dowager in plain clothes, a female paragon in Chinatown, the lady principal of the community's largest Chinese school, the Wah Kun School. Here, my brother and I learned Chinese calligraphy, history, geography, and politics for two hours every day in a building of glass and steel with red trim. We wrote dictation as rat-a-tat Cantonese flowed from our teacher's mouth. We recited paragraphs unhaltingly from thin softcover books with Chinese characters as small as a tiny computer chip written from top to bottom, right to left, books whose covers we rolled and curled and held behind our backs. We grasped our wooden calligraphy brushes upright and swirled black strokes from the inkstone to form graceful words and poetic phrases, the teacher rapping our knuckles if the brush tipped to an angle. Every afternoon at four o'clock for the six years of elementary school, Kent and I walked the one block north on Mott Street to what other Chinese say is the true heart of Chinatown. Wah Kun managed to acquire the status of being Chinatown's architectural centerpiece, and to the unknowledgeable eye, the red crisscrosses of the railings adorning all the windows would seem like Chinese words of good wishes. My brother and I knew that the ×'s and +'s were nothing more than window dressing that made the building a fortress for Auntie Win-Da, dominating as it did over less modern brick walk-ups, our homes.

Auntie Win-Da's demeanor was like the building's, her stature towering over those around her. Her feet glided, they did not step, and the Chinatown pavements never seemed to have garbage where she walked. Her eyes looked straight ahead, never making eye contact with anyone, which would have been unladylike. She never had to carry groceries and instead dangled a purse of stiff black leather with a plastic U-shaped handle from her wrist. When passersby called to her, she merely nodded a greeting. Her silver hair, do not confuse it with gray, was smoothed back from her oval face and high nose and rolled into a French twist that capped her head. Her wonderfully long neck simultaneously pulled up her head and pinned down her shoulders. Auntie Win-Da always wore simple shift dresses, a relaxed collarless version of the Chinese dress, topped with a smart cardigan sweater. Lavender was her favorite color, and it looked vibrant against her porcelain skin. *Everyone* in Chinatown knew who she was and greeted her as if she were the mayor of a small town.

My thoughts are interrupted by Kent when he comes out of his examination room and waves us into the consultation room with him.

To my surprise, a man and a woman are already there.

"Jenny, this is Melinda," Kent was saying. "And this is her father, Mr. Hom. Mr. Hom is a patient of mine."

"Hello, I'm happy to meet you," I say, trying to decide

whose hand to shake first. I aim for Mr. Hom's, age always superceding gender for the Chinese.

Then, as I am shaking Melinda's hand, she says, "Kent's told me a lot about you."

I resist responding that Kent has told me absolutely nothing about her.

"Really? What did he say?"

Melinda glances at Kent, and in that split second, I know that she is not a patient's daughter but a brother's girlfriend.

"Oh, that you're a great sister and an even greater mother. . . . This must be Anni . . . Hi . . ."

Kent turns to Mr. Hom and gives him some last-minute directions for taking the medication he has just prescribed. Melinda and I dance through the initial niceties but Anni is not particularly interested, climbing onto Kent's chair and playing with the colored markers on his desk.

Finally Melinda and her father leave, and I turn to Kent.

"She's nothing like your other girlfriends. Don't you like them chic and sassy, thin and fashionable?"

"But I've never met someone like Melinda," Kent says rapidly. He is well prepared. "She knows a lot about computers and programming . . . she puts up with my obsession with high-end hi-fi equipment . . . she even understands my geeky fishing pals."

"Losing your heart to a heart patient's daughter! Imagine that!" I am trying to sound enthusiastic but only manage to sound sarcastic. "Finally, someone to make you finish renovating your loft." This was all we needed. More changes in the family. "So when are you going to introduce her to Ma Ma and Ba Ba?"

"Sometime soon." Kent sounds uncharacteristically indecisive and distant. But he rebounds quickly.

"Jen, I have to tell you something else about Melinda." I wait.

"Melinda may not be able to have children. She has endometriosis."

Auntie Win-Da's voice comes over the telephone intercom, announcing the next patient. I don't know which has startled me more. I stumble, somehow feeling like I'm standing on my eyelashes, and still, my thoughts go instantly to Ma Ma, and then to the diamond ring. How disgusting, that I should think of that old hurt. "Well, it shouldn't matter if you love her, right?" I say, trying to make up for my secret selfishness. "But what are you going to tell Ma Ma?"

"I don't know. I've got to think about it some more. Anyway, I've got to see these patients now. I'll talk to you soon."

Chinese sons never grow up. They are always between generations, between ancestors and progeny, merely the intermediary, the one who carries on the family name. And now Kent has thrown Melinda into the mix.

Conceived in Hong Kong most probably on the wedding night of our parents, Kent was Ma Ma's secret baggage on her journey to America, traveling with her through Calcutta and Ellis Island. He would become the Chinese-American boy who played stoop ball instead of baseball, marbles instead of football. The splits in the seat of his pants and the holes in the knees proved it.

You could find Kent as a kid across Mott Street at Shea's Soda Fountain, a dark alley of a store owned by Bobby from Little Italy. Kent would be spending a dime on a comic book or a penny on a Bazooka bubble gum or a quarter on a pink Spalding ("Spal-deen") handball. If you couldn't find Kent at Shea's, he might be around the corner on Bayard Street at Rocky's, where dimestore treasures like metal jacks and white chalk and steel skate keys were for sale amid the pots and spatulas and steel scouring pads.

"What is this?" Ba Ba yelled, waving a copy of *A Diary of a Young Girl* by Anne Frank. "What is this junk you're reading?" He was certain this paperback with the black cover and young girl's picture belonged with the *Playboys* and *Mad Magazines* read by all fourteen-year-old boys like Kent.

He had found it among Kent's schoolbooks. Clearly, Ba Ba thought, Kent had been hiding this piece of pornography among his geometry and biology textbooks.

"It's a book I'm reading for school," Kent replied, trying to grab the book back before Ba Ba could damage it. It was a library book.

Kent's desperation seemed to confirm Ba Ba's suspicion. "This is not a schoolbook! You bastard! Fuck your mother's cunt! Don't lie to me!"

So great was Kent's shock at Ba Ba's profanity, a curse that rolls off the tongue of other Chinese men like a harmless verbal tick, a curse never heard before from Ba Ba's lips, that he took two paces back from the living room into the kitchen, and as his hand groped for the cabinet to find his balance, it fell onto the handle of the top drawer, the junk drawer.

"What? Are you trying to kill me? *You* deserve to die!"

Ba Ba pounced on the drawer handle and slid it open, certain Kent was going for a weapon, a screwdriver or pliers or even a ballpoint pen. Ba Ba pulled out the scissors and waved the point at Kent's face.

Ma Ma heard the clash of metal and ran into the kitchen, sliding like a hockey player on the ice onto her knees between them, her hands pulling on Ba Ba's arm with the scissors, pulling the tip down to her bosom. "Kill me instead! Let him be! If you want to kill somebody, kill me instead!"

"So stupid!" he said, waving her off and flinging the book onto the floor. "Damn you all."

Moments later he was stalking down Mott Street to catch the ongoing mah-jongg game.

How will Kent ever tell a mother who took a scissor to her heart that there will be no Liang grandson?

"You're such a Chinese mother," Tomas was fond of saying to me, usually while I was breast-feeding Mark, which was often, at six months, one year, even two years. Tomas meant it lovingly, but it always sounded like criticism, like I was spoiling our son.

When I asked him what he meant, he said, "You're so protective. You think he's so special. . . ."

That was it. He *was* special. I was afraid. For him. And for me. If he is so special, would death find him early? Let me try to explain it as Ma Ma explained it to me. In Ma Ma's village in China, a family was blessed with a son so special that for three consecutive nights before his birth, a single stroke of moonshine streamed into the mother's bedroom window and glowed on her belly. The mother was half-asleep but felt warmth where it should have been cold and knew the stream of white light was not man-made. It was the first decade of the twentieth century, and electricity had not yet discovered these Chinese villages. The mother did not move, not even her lungs or her heart, and she let the warm light bathe her skin and melt into her baby. She had never felt so caressed. The boy was born with hair already cut at the crown into the roundness of a scholar and his eyes were as dark and clear as hematite. The mother carried her baby even before his one-month birthday celebration throughout the village to display to everyone what the heavens had given to her.

"Look at my son," she boasted. "He was blessed by the light of the heaven for three nights before he was born. An angel came to kiss him. The world will one day be his. See, see how special he is!"

On his three-month birthday, the son had a soaring fever for three nights and three days, and on the third night, he fell headfirst into the fever toward death. The angel who had shrouded him with warmth now doused him with cold.

Ma Ma said the light came and kissed the mother's belly for a second time on her second son. Still, the mother had not learned and boasted again, exposing a private message from her gods to the lowly ears of man. The second son died the same as the first. Finally, a third son was conceived, the moon shone, and the mother remained mute for nine months prior to and for sixty-nine years after his birth, when the son had long proven himself as a man with fame far and near, a scholar of letters and a master of inventions. The mother told the story when she herself was ninety years old, secure only then that her story was safe, that her son was safe, from this angel of white light.

My son Mark was born on the fourth day of the second month. If you view it with a Chinese mind, you will see what I mean. The number two, *yee*, sounds exactly the same as the word for "easy," *yee*. The number four in Chinese, *say*, is similar, except in inflection, to the word for "death," *say*. So I knew our son's life was not only special to me, his life was very special to him.

Tomas was much more earthly. A mother with a new baby needs a portable telephone just in case, he said. Just in case I was stuck in traffic. Just in case I ran out of gas. Just in case I wanted to order pizza and have it arrive at home the same time I did. It was a gift that certainly added convenience and safety to my life, and it fit neatly into the bottle pouch of the diaper bag. But I welcomed the telephone most of all for another reason. The number I was assigned had two 2s and three *baat*s, the number eight, which is the luckiest number in Chinese because it rhymes with *faat*, fortune. Tomas never knew how his modern gift served an ancient purpose.

For added good measure, we gave our son three surnames: Marek, after Maria Marek, Tomas's grandmother who raised him in a country farmhouse in the foothills of Eastern Europe while his parents worked in the city. Liang, my maiden name. And Horvath, my married name. Marek Liang Horvath. A name heavy in ancestors, an armor of protection from the lineage of three families. I cannot say anything about moonshine. I can only say my son's life is as masterfully protected as any Chinese male son's.

Chapter Nine

A CUP OR A BOWL

We celebrate Ma Ma's seventy-first birthday about two months later with a party in the lobby at Randal. Adding to our makeshift festivities is the bustle of the newsstand across the way, the tapping sound of footsteps on the red-and-black speckled marble floor, and the swoosh of the revolving doors. As we set up we are like squatters—The Chinese are coming! The Chinese are coming!—with all of our paraphernalia: Anni's stroller, Mark's skateboard, Ma Ma's wheelchair, and, of course, a birthday cake.

Mark wants to push Grand Ma Ma in her wheelchair around the lobby, maybe even have a destination—the newsstand—to buy a pack of gum. We make a train with Grand Ma Ma pushing Anni in her stroller, but the "first car" keeps going awry because of Ma Ma's weak left hand and arm. The fingers of her left hand are perpetually rolled under, spasticity tightening it like a golfer's grip on a club despite Jane Dorsey's red rubber egg. Her curled hand, moist with vinegary "finger jam," rests palm side up on her lap, a lap made too small for bouncing grandchildren by her protruding round belly.

Then Mark comes up with the novel idea of putting his little sister in the giant wheelchair and giving her a ride. Once Ma Ma is seated in one of the molded plastic chairs, she looks on disapprovingly, fearing that Anni will fly out of her wheelchair and get rolled over like an oncoming train. Ma Ma is not enjoying this. The children's laughter is too loud. Their running makes her dizzy. Their ball playing makes her jumpy. We brought Mark's new skateboard to show off his skills on the marble floor but Ma Ma keeps saying, "Be careful! Don't fall! Don't put a hole in your head! Don't do this in the lobby!"

"Come, Ma Ma, let's walk a little," I say, hooking my elbows under Ma Ma's armpits, in hopes of breaking her train of thought and speech. We tango, Ma Ma and I, maybe only five steps, with Ma Ma hobbling on a cane. It is not like bicycle riding after all; one can forget how to walk. Anni joins in, climbing down from the wheelchair and wobbling alongside on her own two feet, making crunchy noises with her diapers and rubbing the corduroy of her overalls.

We let Mark decide how many candles to put on the cake, and he counts eight: one for each decade, plus one for good luck. Anni is given the honor of planting the candles like tulip bulbs into the cake, and she jabs them in extra firmly so that she can lick the icing off her fingers. Ma Ma cannot focus with the commotion of so many hands. As I am trying to get everyone inside the frame of my camera's viewfinder, Vicki starts to wave and Mark starts to jump. Behind me, Kent is coming through the revolving doors, Melinda swirling through behind and then Ba Ba with the *New York Post* under his arm.

After hugs and kisses all around, Kent pauses a bit, and then says, "Ma Ma, this is Melinda. Her father is my patient. Her last name is Hom." He turns toward me and I automatically hand him the matches so that he can busy himself with lighting the candles.

Ma Ma instantaneously focuses her attention on Melinda and beams. She knows Melinda is a serious girl-friend because Kent included her last name. This gives her clues to Melinda's family village in China. "Melinda, I am happy you came."

"Hello, Mrs. Liang, I'm very honored to meet you. Please accept this small gift for your birthday," Melinda says in her fast staccato, with both hands presenting Ma Ma with a slim tie box, her head bowed. Using both hands showed ultimate respect, a gift more appreciated by Ma Ma than the contents in the box. Ma Ma lets Anni tear off the gift wrap and even lets her pull out the red paisley chal-lis shawl. Both Melinda and I drape it around Ma Ma's shoulders, and before I can compliment Ma Ma's beauty and Melinda's good taste, Melinda has already whisked the box and paper away and dunked it into the garbage bin, as efficient as Ma Ma.

Ba Ba misses the episode with the challis shawl. He is sitting catty-corner to us like a benched player on the sidelines.

"What are you learning in school, Vicki?" Ba Ba asks. He seems sincerely interested although his eyes are glittering on Mark pushing Anni again in the wheelchair, with gaiety and abandon and in circles. Ba Ba never seems to find his grandchildren stressful, and they always find him dear. So does our dog Max.

"Oh, I'm studying everything, Grand Ba Ba," Vicki is saying. Like Ba Ba who always has a newspaper, Vicki always has a novel or textbook she is reading or studying. She shows him Camus's *The Stranger*, and they put their heads together to read a page.

"It's about a man who doesn't belong," Vicki says quietly, "a man who feels out of place everywhere...."

Our little birthday party suddenly seems absurd, as though we are in an airport lounge waiting for a plane that will never arrive.

"Thank you, Melinda, the scarf is very pretty," Ma Ma says, strongly and clearly, putting us back on track. She takes hold of Melinda's hand and I snap my camera at this new photo opportunity. "Tell me, where are you from?"

"Queens, Mrs. Liang. My parents are from Toishan." Melinda sits down next to Ma Ma, her arms over the chrome armrest as she uses her two hands to cradle Ma Ma's one. They look oddly like mother and daughter, the same square jaw, the same body shape and height.

"Ohhh, that's good," Ma Ma says. "I have many relatives living in Toishan. And how old are you?"

"Twenty-seven years, Mrs. Liang."

"And working?"

"Yes, Mrs. Liang, I am a computer programmer for a small company uptown."

Kent, not unaware of Ma Ma's questions, was explaining to Mark why the farthest candles should be lit first. He could not have brought a better birthday present for Ma Ma. Most important, Melinda is young and able, to work and to mother.

For Ma Ma's birthday, Tomas and I give her a couple of *hoong bows* and a dozen oranges, the symbol of life—that which bears fruit—and sweetness, in one of those ubiquitous orange plastic bags from a Chinatown street vendor.

"Oranges," Ma Ma says, holding one with a pretty navel, nostalgia making her eyes wet. "We roll oranges on the bed of newlyweds to wish them a fruitful marriage."

I look over to Kent, who is pretending to give orders to Mark and Anni as though they were nurses. He is looking too busy so I know he is listening.

"Do you know what a fruitful marriage is, Melinda?" Ma Ma continues.

"No, Mrs. Liang, what is it?" Melinda is being very polite and very smart. She knows all the right things to say.

"A fruitful marriage is one with children, Melinda."

"Ma Ma, let me peel the orange for you," I interrupt. I squeeze and rotate it in my hand, giving it an undeserved study. Then I rip off the ragged rind, turning my fingers white and sticky with the oil, and pull the strands of zest as I would lint on a sweater. Ma Ma eyes me the way an artist views a slob.

Her silence says many words.

This is offending her, butchering this orange as I am, without knife or plate or finesse. She has served me, our family, scores of oranges on birthdays and New Year's, delicately slipping the point of the knife in the center of its underside and sliding down to the opposite pole to make perfectly even triangular pieces of peel. Pulling each sliver back and stacking them on the plate, she then picked the individual threads of zest like a seamstress embroidering and piled them into a web. Only then was the orange, this highly revered fruit, this symbol of the only acceptable marriage, ready to be opened, each wedge lined up like Radio City Rockettes on a plate before being slipped into the mouth.

"All right, Mark, you can light one," Kent is saying. "Just one, though." He holds Mark's hand and flips the matchbook flap back. "Press tightly here, then pull." The match snaps alive and Mark's face opens with delight. I hurry behind my camera again, glad I don't have to sing in my offkey voice, but I hear Melinda. She sings at a fast clip, a half beat ahead of everyone.

"Ba Ba, have another piece of cake," I offer.

"No, thank you. One is enough."

Melinda cuts the cake cleanly with the small plastic knife while I snap more photos. Ma Ma picks around the buttercream frosting and eats only the carrot cake, while the kids do the opposite. Melinda and I both want seconds, and I realize I am beginning to like her. I make a mental note to get a duplicate set of photos for her. Then it occurs to me I may need a third set to start a progress book for Ma Ma like the baby books I have created for Vicki, Mark, and Anni.

I continue clicking my camera, trying to get Ma Ma and Anni together in the same frame but having great difficulty with Anni so mobile and Ma Ma so stationary. The viewfinder becomes my eye, and I chase after Anni with it but find Auntie Win-Da walking toward us. I quickly check the cake to see whether I need to give up my second slice.

"Auntie, how happy we are to see you today," I say, handing her my plate.

"This is Melinda, Win *jeah jeah*," Ma Ma says, wasting no time pointing out the most important feature of the day.

"Yes, Melinda, nice to see you. How is your father?" Auntie Win-Da says with the smoothness of familiarity.

"Father is fine, thank you," Melinda replies.

Ma Ma's look matches her mouthful of cake. She has already swallowed life whole, damn the stroke, and whatever she could not get down was still in her mouth. How much of life is passing her by?

"Do you know Melinda?" she asks Auntie Win-Da.

"Yes, of course, Melinda is a very caring daughter," Auntie Win-Da says carefully. "She accompanies her father on all of his visits to Dr. Liang."

"Is that so? Melinda, Melinda, let me ask you a riddle." Ma Ma turns, and asks as if she were a game-show host. "Let's say both Kent and I were in a burning building. Whom would you save?" I have heard these verbal mother-in-law tricks before when Ma Ma explained how Great-Auntie Moy had handpicked the woman for her son in an arranged marriage.

I knew the wrong answer. Don't ever say, "I don't know, it's a difficult question to answer."

Melinda thinks for a moment, and says, "Oh, I'm young and strong. I can save you both."

I look over at Kent. Smart brother. He'd prepared her.

Ma Ma glows and goes on to question number two. "Melinda, I love to eat chicken. Do you? Which part do you prefer, white meat or dark meat?"

This riddle seems so innocent, but don't ever say,

"White meat, definitely. I like chicken breast much more than drumsticks."

Melinda avoids the pitfall. "Mrs. Liang, I like everything. I eat whatever is placed in front of me."

Finally, Ma Ma holds up her cake plate. "Melinda, what do you think? Is this a cup or a bowl?"

Kent and I know there is no right answer, only the best answer.

Melinda goes for three out of three. "It is whichever you say, Mrs. Liang."

Melinda passes.

Chapter Ten

A CHINAMAN'S CHANCE

$\mathcal{B}$a Ba's temper had always moved in like summer tornadoes, emotional twisters that formed out of nothing and dissipated into nothing.

"Open the door! Open the door!" Ba Ba had often banged at Kent's office door. "Where's Kent? I need Kent. I'm sick! Tell Kent I need him!" The patients cowered in their seats at the noise even as they stretched their necks to see who was creating this drama.

"Where's Ma? I'm going to kill her. She stole all my money."

"She's putting poison in my food. She's trying to kill me."

Now, since Ma Ma's stroke, the storms that were passing through him grew worse. His confusion became dangerous. The smoke detectors beeped all too often.

Staring at the blackened pot: "Oh, I forgot the water was boiling."

Holding up scorched pants: "Who left the iron on?"

The sink overflowing onto his shoes: "Why was the water running?"

"Who left the TV on through the night?"

Finally, Ba Ba's confusion melted into despair.

The note he slipped under Kent's office door read: "Please come see me. I'm dying. Your father."

Ba Ba and Ma Ma had started to live separately the year before, Ba Ba on the second floor in a one-bedroom apartment, number 22, Ma Ma still in the first-floor apartment in which we had grown up. We hired a live-in housekeeper to care for Ba Ba—Donna, who was referred to us by Kent's parking lot attendant in Chinatown. She had shoulders strong and broad enough to carry me across them like a yoke for two water buckets. She was a grandmother at age fifty and said she preferred taking care of "big babies" over "little babies." For a few months it all seemed to be working out well. But then both Ba Ba and Donna fell sick at the same time and had to be taken to the emergency room at Bankford Hospital. When Kent arrived, he was told that Ba Ba had only a passing stomach bug, not to worry, but the housekeeper had a much more serious heart condition.

It turned out that it had been Ba Ba taking care of Donna all along—cooking and cleaning for her. And he had enjoyed being needed.

Now with Ma Ma at Randal and Ba Ba home alone, I saw matchmaking possibilities, unable to abandon my need to get their marriage right, to get Ma Ma and Ba Ba together, if not on their terms at least on mine. I wanted that diamond ring.

"I am going to ask Ba Ba to come live with us," I say to Ma Ma during one afternoon visit.

"*Ai*, you're mad!" she exclaims. I have never seen her muscles so alive, so animated with the desire to leap from her wheelchair and punctuate what she is saying. "He will stir chaos into your family."

Ba Ba had seen Ma Ma the night before her stroke, he in his bathrobe and she in hers. He had pounded on her apartment door sometime before midnight, a nightly ritual.

"Open the door!" Standing in his slippers, Ba Ba tried to roar above the echoing sound of his fist on the fireproof, burglarproof steel door. "Kent! Where are you?"

He waited and pounded, waited and pounded, sometimes for as long as half an hour, until Ma Ma opened the door, startled awake from her sleep. They stood slipper to slipper.

"What do you want?" Ma Ma said derisively. "Go back to sleep."

"I'm sick. I need help. I need Kent," he screamed. "Call him. Call him to come here."

"Kent is not here. You're out of your mind," she said. "Go away."

If only ... if only Ba Ba would take my kids fishing in Central Park. I know exactly how it would be. He would pack up slices of Wonder bread for bait and wear his khaki cap and shorts with plenty of pockets. They would venture, the four of them, by subway from the Canal Street station, the unofficial border between Chinatown and the Rest of the World. And they would feel a summer temperature debriefing, their bodies cooling underground where their nasal Chinese voices echoed and the air turned blue.

They would be Chinese Huck Finns, a gangly Chinese grandfather with three children tagging along, holding fishing poles and a purple pail.

"We want to go on a rowboat," Vicki would start.

"And I want to row," Mark would continue.

"Me, too," Anni would follow.

"Fishing is better from the shore," Grand Ba Ba would say.

"But it's too hot today," Mark would reason.

They would not breathe until Grand Ba Ba said, "All right. We can row for one hour."

They would give up a quiet cheer as they skipped along winding paths through Central Park, past the smell of the seals' pool and the sounds of the polar bear cave, past the musical carousel with the gold ring, the grand shell of the bandstand, down the row of high stairs to the cobble-stoned fountain facing the lake. They would stop at the steps on the shore and ask any sitting fisherman, "Are they biting today?" Mark would be wowed by the big catfish that would squirm to the surface at the end of his line, but he would have to throw it back.

"Their bellies are filthy," Grand Ba Ba would say. "They clean the bottom of the lake."

My kids would sit for hours holding fishing rods with tips Grand Ba Ba had carved from bamboo chopsticks, a dime a pair from Ma Ma's shop, tapering them to flex with the gentlest nibble but strong enough to pull back on any fierce tug. The handle would be made from a bundle wrapped again and again with embroidery cord into finally what could be the grasp of a samurai sword. They would communicate to each other by watching the bobbing red-and-white plastic buoys, an enchanting Morse code between generations.

Kent and I call another limited family executive meeting, this time with Ba Ba but without Ma Ma. Like board members, neither Kent nor I know each other's position on the issue. We invite Ba Ba to a Chinatown restaurant for dinner, one that specializes in seafood because eating steamed flounder in black bean sauce and sautéed crabs in sea salt is like going to a fifteen-course wedding banquet, and we want time for a good meal and, if need be, a good fight.

Ba Ba keeps his head down as he drinks his soup, a hybrid eggdrop corn chowder. It is the first dinner ever that is just the three of us. Without the clatter of the children, Ba Ba senses this dinner will not be just eating.

I cannot wait until he finishes his soup. "Ba Ba, how do you like living alone?" I ask. "What do you need?"

He continues his concentration on his porcelain soup spoon with the trough handle, catching the kernels of corn into its ladle. "It's not so bad. You don't have to worry about me. . . ."

"But we do. We worry about you, Ba," Kent says, in a tone somewhere between the college prep he once was and the medical sophisticate he now is, ever handsome in his cashmere sweater and thin-striped shirt.

"That's right. We worry you're not eating right, you might hurt yourself, you're lonely. . . ." I say. I sound so much like a mother.

"So? So what can you do?" Ba Ba says. This time he

stops and rests his spoon upside down on the edge of his bowl. He moves his eyes sideways to peer out the side of his glasses, which are a little fogged from the steam of the soup.

"So you can come and live with us," I answer.

"No, he can't live with you," Kent says too quickly.

"No, I can't live with you," Ba Ba repeats immediately. Had they planned their responses? Had they conspired with Ma Ma?

"Jenny, you have your children," Ba Ba says. "You take care of them. What do you need me for? I'm an old man. I'll get in your way. You'll get in my way. And," he even laughs, "what if I set your house on fire?"

My eyes prickle with tears, and I am not even drinking soup. "You have nowhere to go. You have no choice."

Platters of seafood arrive. I half expect Ba Ba to drizzle the thin stream of ocher oil over everything. I miss it that he doesn't.

"Yes, he does," Kent says, being the first to lay in the chopsticks, not to serve himself but to break off the floun-der tail and hoist it to Ba Ba's plate. I ladle a spoonful of the "fish juice" with black beans and diced scallions and pour it onto the tail.

"Ba Ba does have a choice. Maybe a pretty good one," Kent is saying as he tugs at a crab leg. "How about living in a nursing home, Ba Ba? You know, where you live with a lot of people and they take care of you."

Ba Ba carefully picks around the bones, especially the jelly cartilage lining the sides of the fish, pushing two-inch slabs into his mouth and pulling out the bones, one by one. Is he listening as carefully?

"There's a nursing home on Staten Island, Ba Ba, with mostly Chinese residents," Kent continues. "Many of my patients live there. You'll have friends, you can watch TV, you can go for walks. They even have a nurse who lives there in case of emergency."

Kent pauses as he plops a particularly plump crab on my plate, then takes a lean one for himself. Such is the Chinese way. Such is a big brother.

"I've been thinking about that, too," Ba Ba says. "I just want everyone to relax about me. *I* want to relax about me. It's enough that you take care of Ma Ma."

Whatever happened to "so stupid"? "Yes, we will take care of Ma Ma. But we must take care of you, too."

"I know, Jenny. I know what you want to do. You want to do everything. But sometimes you can't. Sometimes, no matter how hard you try, you just can't."

Ba Ba puts down his chopsticks, takes off his glasses, and wipes his forehead with the dinner napkin.

"When I first came to America, they used to say, 'You don't stand a Chinaman's chance.' Good thing they don't say that anymore!"

And then he smiles.

"This nursing home idea. It is probably the best solution for all of us, for you two, for Jenny's children, for Ma Ma. . . ."

"But what about you?" I say. "How will you like living with a lot of people? How will you like living outside of Chinatown?"

He smiles again, and I think of Dr. Cheng and his big house.

"Just make sure I get all the newspapers."

We eat, speaking no longer, not unlike most Chinese who slurp and shove food at mealtimes without conversation. Such a reverence for food we nourished. Ba Ba meticulously picks through the prized head only aficionados appreciate and although he seems to be giving it his entire attention, his mind is wandering. Pulling a bone from between his lips with his chopsticks, Ba Ba seems to start midsentence, "Remember last summer when we went to Kent's weekend house, in the country, in Upstate New York?" He stops eating altogether. "That was one of the best days of my life. We went fishing. It was at the lake behind the house. By the end of the day, we had a pile of fish and we felt so good. We had chicken on the barbecue and we didn't burn it, not even the soy sauce and honey on the skin. Jenny's kids were running around, spraying everyone and the cars with the water hose. You know, if you don't live long enough, you don't get to see it. But if you live too long, you can't appreciate it. Right now, I feel just right."

Chapter Eleven

"TANK U"

It is the fifteenth Tuesday of Ma Ma's stay at Randal. I have been ticking off the days on our kitchen calendar, the same calendar we use to note exams and school dances for Vicki in blue marker, playdates and birthday parties for Mark in red, and doctor's appointments for Anni in pink. Ma Ma was added in green. No one knows how long Ma Ma will stay at Randal but we all sense her departure is imminent. Tonight, I come late to visit Ma Ma because of an evening parent-teacher conference at Mark's nursery school. He is doing superbly, I was told, bringing an energy to his class that was sorely missed whenever he was absent. On Ma Ma's progress, I was getting periodic casual reports from Jane Dorsey, catch as catch can. Tony and Mrs. Sampson corroborated that Ma Ma was the model patient.

"Your mother never complains," said Mrs. Sampson.

"She's always so polite. She says 'tank u, tank u' all the time," said Tony.

"She's getting stronger," said Jane Dorsey.

Ma Ma got straight A's for effort, attitude, and willingness. When Mark's teacher said he was an all-round A student, I said, Of course. But hearing Mrs. Sampson, Tony, and Jane Dorsey rave about Ma Ma, I was skeptical. Ma Ma was able to camouflage most of her emotional staleness, a weariness that was evident to me when she sits in her wheelchair looking out her twelfth-floor window. Was she reminiscing about kite flying in Hong Kong? About chop-chopping dinner for us in a kitchen smelling of photographic solution? Was she thinking about Vicki leaving home for college sometime soon? Dreaming about Kent's marriage and a new grandson? What grade would she get for memories? For her future?

It is after dinnertime for Ma Ma when I arrive, myself having just wolfed down a dinner of sesame-seed bagel and cream cheese and chocolate milk in the car coming directly from Mark's school. I pant into Ma Ma's room gnawed by a rush to get home to Anni, but when Ma Ma is neither sitting in her wheelchair by the window nor lying in her bed, my panting turns into panic. My imagination jumps ahead into a classic Hollywood heart stopper. My god, did they take the body away already?

I suddenly realize the entire floor is rather empty of patients and the flickering fluorescent lights are actually noisy. Clothes are thrown on beds, closet doors are left open, chairs are not pushed up against the wall. Everyone has left in a hurry. It looks like the remnants of a fire drill.

I hastily round the corner outside of Ma Ma's room and ask at the nurse's station.

"Oh, everyone is in class. Your mom's downstairs in the clubroom," a nurse tells me. "I think it's basket weaving tonight."

She must be joking, I think, the way army sergeants tell new recruits they're all ladies and should wear tutus and take up knitting. I head to the clubroom, suspicion swiftly replacing anxiety, as though I will catch Ma Ma on a date or some other illicit activity. Somehow this is more bizarre to me than Ma Ma eating gelatin.

The clubroom, long, narrow, and harsh, is very much like the conference room in the advertising company where we had pitched many a campaign to clients, except this table is Formica and the dozen or so molded plastic chairs are piled in one corner so that everyone sits at the table in a wheelchair. Ma Ma is at the far end, near the front of the room, second from the teacher. She looks small and cute in the distance, and I can tell she is one of the teacher's favorites. Ma Ma smiles and waves for me to come sit behind her, and I pull up a chair to peer over her shoulder. She is teetering her basket in her lap, the thin wire frame wobbling in her left hand, barely managing to thread another yellow plastic "yarn" up and down one of the posts at the base of the basket and pull it through. The trick is holding the basket tightly with her left hand, a grip she has been strengthening with the red rubber egg. Now finally it all makes sense.

Ma Ma proudly holds up her half-naked basket to show me, and I nod my head and tap her shoulder. "Very pretty," I say. She pulls the yellow yarn around the oval frame and then the orange yarn to layer hideously above the yellow one. Yellow and orange. My god, my mother has become such a child.

"Here, it is for you." She gives me the basket when it is done the following week. "Don't let Kent know I gave it to you. I don't have one for him."

Our kitchen calendar sports a big green heart in the box marked August 1. Ma Ma's homecoming. She will be starting anew. My heart warms as I think of Vicki, who must have had some sort of foresight when she gave up her bedroom to share one with Mark. That room will now be Ma Ma's. I tackle my new project with my organizer in hand.

But few department stores and mail-order catalogs sell beds and tables and lamps for a mother felled by a stroke. There is no special "layette" for Ma Ma as there were for my homecoming babies. So I improvise, starting with the bed. We dismantle Vicki's and Mark's bunk beds and give Ma Ma the top half with its removable railings on both sides. The top bunk, placed on the floor, will be like her adult crib, even down to the fleece-lined rubber mat under the fitted sheet in case she soils the bed.

"Are you sleeping well?" I had asked Ma Ma.

"Sleeping okay," she had lied. The unfamiliar had always kept her awake all her life and now it seemed nothing was familiar. There was the new medication the nurse just gave to her; a new roommate due the next day; a new resident who would examine her; a friend coming to visit.

"Can you turn in the night?" How do you do that when half of you is disabled?

"Yes," she said, "but to say the truth, I am afraid of falling out of bed."

Once the bed was resolved, and its solution came easily, I imagined the rest would fall into place. I plunge into the Yellow Pages and find F & G Surgical a few towns north of ours. It turns out to be a no-frills hospital-supply warehouse, a shoebox of glass and aluminum stocked with digital thermometers and blood-pressure instruments of all sorts and plastic pill cases of all sizes. The dust immediately flecks across my eyes in the sunshine coming through the glass and I feel I have entered the Starship *Enterprise* for the Infirm. The years of dirt on the plastic bags covering the assortment of goods gives everything a film of horror. I quickly pick up from a rack on the counter two metal "dog tag" bracelets to warn emergency medics of the wearer's health problems, one that reads "diabetes" for Ma Ma and another with "contact lenses" for me.

A man with an unlit cigar between his lips squeezes out from his office mess of piled invoices and manila folders. "What can I do you for?" he asks, noting the goods in my hands.

I have clearly interrupted him, but I push on. "I need some supplies for my mother. She had a stroke." The words are thick and squinting, and even now, I must cough to clear them, to say the four simple words. I blink; it must be the dust and sunlight to blame. But having said that to him, a stranger, uncaring and possibly hostile, I feel some hold deep within me loosen and I am able to breathe to that point once again.

"Okay, what do you need?" the man demands.

"I don't know," I begin helplessly, knowing that I am annoying him. I take a stab at it: "How about a toilet seat?" Anni is just starting her potty training, and the topic has been prominent in my mind.

"What kind?" he asks.

A toilet seat is a toilet seat. What does he mean, what kind?

Without waiting for an answer, he pulls out an aluminum chair with a sunken pan in its plastic seat and clunks it down in front of me.

"Two hundred dollars," he says. I don't even have to ask.

Then he hooks down a plastic toilet seat from the wall with the kind of brass-tipped long wooden rod my elementary school teacher used to pull open the high windows. "This kind you put on top of a toilet. Six inches high. Sixty dollars. How high do you need?"

How high do I need? *How high a toilet seat do I need?* So stupid! How should I know the exact science of toilet seats and the highness of the prices? Is a higher seat a higher price?

"I don't know," I say again.

He puts the seat in my hands and I am surprised at how big and awkward and heavy it is, especially compared to Anni's miniature potty.

He hooks down another toilet seat. "Eight inches. With handles at the sides. Eighty dollars." Ten dollars an inch, I think. This one is lighter plastic, though.

"This one, I think," keeping the eight-incher in my hands. Ma Ma will like the sidebars. And she will not have to bend down so low nor hoist up so high.

Next: a shower chair. I imagined all sorts of Houdini contraptions to enable Ma Ma to climb in and out over the bulky bathtub ledge, but nothing like what the smokeless cigar man puts down in front of me: one chair that looks like a bridge chair of sturdy ivory plastic with holes the size of golf balls in the seat and in the back. The feet have large rubber suction cups at the bottom for slip-proof operation. Ninety dollars.

The second chair is two in tandem, like a motor scooter with a companion buggy seat at the side, with a total of six legs and suctioned feet. The main chair has a seat and back of padded vinyl.

"This part goes on the floor outside the tub," the man says, pointing to the bench side with two legs. "The chair and the four legs go inside the tub. So she sits here on the bench and slides over to the chair into the tub."

Clever as Houdini. "How much is this one?"

"One hundred fifty dollars."

Ma Ma will never be able to manage with the single chair. "Okay, this big one. Will it fit in the trunk?"

"Sure. You can unscrew it here and here. And if you need new cushions, you can replace them by unscrewing these."

But new cushions? Will Ma Ma outlast her shower chair?

I have just spent two hundred thirty dollars in the last ten minutes for only two items. I need something small.

"How about one of these pill organizers?" I point into the glass counter.

He takes out a long slim box with a sliding top and three compartments about one inch square each. It looks like one of Ba Ba's fishing-tackle boxes but it is obvious this is for one day's medication, morning, noon, and night. He then takes out a large square box with a grid of cubes, enough for a week's worth. Three times seven equals twenty-one squares. I like this one, too, because it is red. Ma Ma will be happy taking pills from this box. Besides, filling the box once a week will be more convenient.

"Fifteen dollars," he says. Actually I like his efficiency. We are beginning to understand each other.

"I think my mother will like one of those raised cushions for sleeping," I say, pointing to the shelf.

"How high?"

Oh, no. I make one up. "Six inches."

"This one's regular foam. Thirty dollars. This one's contoured foam. Forty-five dollars."

Regular foam is good enough. And she can elevate her feet too.

"Now, how about handrails? I need one outside the bathroom, one next to the toilet, and one by the bed."

He shows me small, medium, and large, what look like a foot long, twenty inches, and thirty inches. I expect the handrails to be oversized towel racks, but these are industrial-size and industrial-gauge aluminum that are too heavy and thick for simply hanging terry cloth. Total cost: eighty dollars.

Finally, I am ready to tackle a wheelchair.

"Well, this here is the Rolls-Royce. It's motorized. Just push this joystick," he says. "And the front wheels pivot almost forty-five degrees both ways so you have real control."

Very nice, I think, but this is way over Ma Ma's head. The speed and spinning would make her carsick. The joystick would frighten her. "I need something simpler, small but comfortable. Our apartment isn't too big."

"This one's good quality. It'll last you. Sturdy frame. Thick canvas seat and back," he says. I watch him wheel out another chair.

I sit in the wheelchair, feeling as close as I have ever physically felt to being in Ma Ma's situation. She would have been horrified. *Dai gut lai see.* "It's bad luck," she had scolded Mark and Anni when they climbed into her chair for fun. "Come down!" Abruptly I stand up, trying to imagine the fit of this chair for Ma Ma. She must be about twenty or thirty pounds heavier than me but not much wider. Most of her extra weight is in her belly. This is a medium-sized chair. The man pulls his sagging pants by his belt over his belly about the size of Ma Ma's, showing his impatience again at my distractions and indecisiveness. Damn, he just doesn't get it. I catch myself not breathing again, the dust getting in my eyes.

He quickly interrupts any emotions of mine that might be surfacing.

"How much do you want to spend?" he asks. The price range is quite wide, I am told. A modest wheelchair costs about five hundred dollars and the Rolls-Royce is two thousand dollars. I choose the "good quality" one, the one I sat in, the way I would choose a mattress, bouncing on it to feel the firm support and great construction. "Best value for the money," he adds. Eight hundred fifty dollars.

That was without a seat cushion. I choose one that is covered in black vinyl to match the black canvas of the chair, a four-inch-thick cushion with a large V cut out toward the back to afford Ma Ma comfort to her tailbone. Well, at least this was well thought out. I never would have thought of that. I never thought I would spend over one thousand two hundred dollars either.

The man does not forget to add in the two bracelets and he doesn't help me carry a thing to the car, not even the bracelets or the pill box. I particularly do not like his brown pants. It takes me three trips and a lot of figuring to get everything to fit, and I am glad for all the times I played the computer game Tetris with Mark. As I squeeze the toilet seat in between the shower chair legs, I am thinking what a relief it is not to have to buy a bedpan. At least Ma Ma won't be needing that.

Finally I confront Ma Ma's old clothes. They need to be cleared out and given away, and I charge into the project like a professional personal shopper picking out the do's and don'ts in her closet.

In Ma Ma's empty apartment one afternoon, I open her chestnut-brown wardrobe, and my favorite dress on Ma Ma catches my eye and my hand first. The fabric feels like gauze, but with a sheen, in sea-blue and green swirls. The fashionable would call the color "foam," and on Ma Ma, her skin inherited an extra layer of luminosity. I remember insisting that she wear it, with its matching short bolero jacket, to our Mother's Day dinner a few years ago. She insisted that blue and green were not festive enough to wear, that she must wear something in red, and we compromised when I presented her with a corsage of miniature salmon roses. There is foam coming into my eyes as I slip the dress and the jacket off the hangers and coarsely fold them into thirds, first against my chest, then my waist, and finally my knees. I bend down and drop them into a large black garbage bag, hearing the gauze rustle against the plastic as it peels apart. *Lop sop* again.

My eyes are gauze now and my brain stuffed with cotton as I continue to empty Ma Ma's closet, first gathering the more official-looking gray-and-gold floral dress with the blazer, then the aqua dress with tiny white dots Ma Ma didn't like because it gave her skin a rash patina. Yes, yes, carry on, Jenny, the ladies at the senior citizen center now housed in P.S. 23, my old elementary school, on Bayard Street will put these dresses to good use. I start to fold blindly, ignoring the fact that this dress was another of Ma Ma's favorites (see how worn through under the arms it is?) and that I had chosen this fabric (see the telltale modern geometric pattern?). It comes over me out of a new darkness of premonition that one day I will be doing this again for a different, more final reason.

Her home is empty and silent, the late afternoon filling it with a lightless gray. Closing the heavy metal door behind me, I glance over at the dumbwaiter where you could still see the charred bricks, the faint stars, if you know where to look.

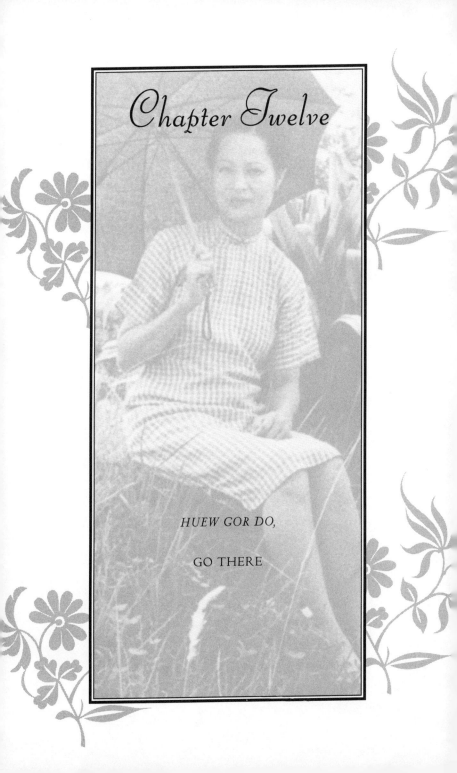

Chapter Twelve

HUEW GOR DO,

GO THERE

*J*enny, this isn't a Best Daughter in the World competition!" Kent is screaming and cannot be a bigger bully.

"You have no idea, Kent, no idea what I've gone through to get this room ready for Ma Ma!" The English green paint has been covered with a rose pink. The carpeting has been pulled up, leaving a bare wood floor. Handrails have been anchored to the wall. A hand shower, European style, has been added to the tub faucet in the adjoining bathroom.

We are standing at the doorway of what was to be Ma Ma's new room, crowded like pork-belly traders in the Stock Exchange on Wall Street, our voices too loud and too close and our breaths too misty and too fishy. We have just finished a paella brunch, Liang-style with Chinese sausages, in celebration of Vicki's high school graduation and college acceptance. I had gotten giant prawns from the Fish Guy, our restaurant wholesaler, especially for Ba Ba, and had been careful not to make the rice mushy, especially for Ma Ma.

"Jenny, you were smart to leave the shells on," Ba Ba says as he comes for seconds. I pick out the extra big prawns for him. "It gives everything more flavor, you know."

I notice that Ba Ba has gained a little weight.

"But Ma Ma won't like living in the suburbs," Kent continues. "She will be most comfortable in Chinatown. That's home to her. She's used to everything there: the air, the noises, the food. You can't just uproot her."

"Well, we uprooted Ba Ba, didn't we?"

Kent is unfazed. "I've already made the arrangements."

"What do you mean, *arrangements*? That sounds so final!"

"I've talked to the therapists and doctors at Randal. And I've found someone who will take care of her and live with her."

"But we agreed Ma Ma would come live with me!"

"We said let's see how it goes."

"And that means to you, Kent, let *you* decide!"

"It's the best for her." Kent is not letting up.

"How do *you* know what's best for her, or for me? You just make all the decisions without consulting anyone. I can't stand it anymore! I don't need this! I don't need any of you! Get out!"

How un-Chinese of me. People are never thrown from houses. Only bad gods are.

"We don't want her to leave." Jane Dorsey laughs. "She's our best patient. Right, Mrs. Liang?"

"You are best, Jane Dorsey." Ma Ma laughs, too, but her eyes are complacent and eager.

"Thank you, but you really are the ideal. You always do what you're told. You never complain. You even eat most of your food!" I look at Mrs. Sampson to see if she is being sarcastic.

"Food is good," Ma Ma says. She's got to be kidding. All these months, she has been longing for me to bring her food from Chinatown, white containers of beef and bok choy or roast pork and bean curd over rice. But I wouldn't. You should get used to the food here, I said. I marked off the menu daily with food choices for her. She retaliated by never eating everything on her plate. Imagine that. Leaving leftovers.

"We'll miss you. Good luck, Mrs. Liang," they say together.

"Good luck, good luck," Ma Ma repeats, the way she used to end every phone call with me. "Good luck, good luck, good luck," she had said the night before her stroke, always leaving every conversation on a happy thought.

Now she's leaving Randal on a happy thought. But I am hard put to share it.

"Ma Ma, come live with me," I said again and again.

"You love me, Jenny, I know," Ma Ma kept saying. "But I cannot live with you—or with Kent."

This infuriates me. This was not the deal at all. I know that somehow Kent is to blame, though I can't put my finger on exactly how.

"Why not? We can take care of you, like how you used to take care of me."

"No, Jenny, remember Yee Ma, my sister? She had six children and didn't live with any one of them. Why?

Because she loved them. She had her own apartment with a housekeeper. Many housekeepers. And they always complained about what a difficult woman Yee Ma was. She was *so* picky. The weather was always too hot or too cold. Her apartment was always too noisy or too lonely. Even rice had to be cooked exactly her way: washed three times, water level measured to the first knuckle on the pinky finger, steam covered for twenty minutes. All of her children would share these stories and just laugh. They wouldn't laugh if she were living with them. That way is the best way.

"Jenny, don't worry about me," Ma Ma said again and again. "You take care of your family. Everything will take care of itself."

"*You* don't worry," I shot back.

And so it came to be.

Ma Ma is on her way home some two hundred days after the fall in the night, making the round-trip journey to the same address where she had come with her two-suitcase dowry forty years ago, to learn life over again. It was by all measures an expedition more fraught than her maiden voyage from China to America. This time, she was neither pregnant with expectation nor with my brother, but her body was at the aftermath of a personal 7.2 earthquake, her physical structure and emotional foundations crumbled and detached. Her stroke had leveled her to the absolute necessity of accepting what others must do for her, however and whichever way it was done.

I arranged to have Ma Ma discharged on Tony's day off, and he takes the ride downtown with us. She comes home on his strong arm like a soldier coming home from war and a war bride combined.

"Hello, Mrs. Liang! You're coming home," the neighbors yell to Ma Ma as she sits in the front seat of the car waiting for Tony to come around like a chauffeur with her wheelchair. Why do Chinese always say the obvious?

"Yes, I am home now," Ma Ma says through the open car door. More neighbors and some strangers start to crowd around, out of homecoming spirit and out of sheer nosiness. So *this* is what happened to Mrs. Liang, they are thinking. We haven't seen her for so long that we thought she was . . . So *this* is what happens when you have a stroke. But she can speak. She's not a mute. I can feel the collective relief.

"You can talk!" says Mrs. Moy, the fifth-floor neighbor who was holding a few plastic orange bags bursting with groceries. Why are Chinese so blunt?

"Of course I can talk." Ma Ma looks sharply at her. Her fire is still there. And she isn't embarrassed to have a white man, Tony, holding her hand and helping her swing her legs out of the car on display in Chinatown. "Tank u, Tony." Ma Ma turns her attention to him, her face right next to his now, letting him put her right hand on the top ledge of the car door to pull herself up to a half-standing position. He wraps his arm around her back, letting her right arm drop to his shoulders, and he moves in one motion to swirl her into the wheelchair.

"Oh, you are all so busy. Good-bye! Come visit me when you have time," Ma Ma says to signal that the show is over. The neighbors go off with something they can talk about for the next couple of days.

Ma Ma crosses the sidewalk in her wheelchair. To the right where there was once a dry goods store is now a grocery store, Wing Fan, selling greens like bok choy from crates and thousand-year-old eggs from large brown ceramic pots the urban chic use as planters. To the left, on the other side of a basement Chinese restaurant with the unlikely German name, the Rathskeller, is no longer the souvenir shop that was our major competitor, but two stalls, one hawking T-shirts and the other, baseball caps. Across Mott Street where Shea's used to be, a coffeehouse, Hai Tong, stands with only three tables seating four each. It is always filled with the noise of old Chinese men exchanging news from Off Track Betting in the smoke of their Lucky Strikes over coffee made rich and clear by the eggshells added to the grind, coffee they slurped from a spoon, and *cha sui bows*, roast pork in steamed white buns.

Tony's strength manages to back Ma Ma in her wheelchair up the front steps, the same steps Ba Ba once sat on waiting for Mr. Chin and Mr. Lee to call him home. Tony rolls her down the hallway and says at the foot of the stairs, "Okay, Mrs. Liang, show us how much you've learned, how strong your legs are." They are standing in front of apartment number 12, where Ma Ma had raised her family, where Ba Ba had banged on her door in the middle of the night, where she had fallen close to dawn.

She pauses. Tony thinks it is because of the formidable ten steps ahead of her, but she is paying tribute to this place of her past. A silent prayer passes her lips as though she were standing at a gravesite.

"Come on, Mrs. Liang. Don't be afraid. I'll help you." Tony folds his arm around her back and over to her armpit, hoisting her up. "Remember, up with the good leg." I pull the wheelchair from under her, bend down to push the safety latch, and squeeze the handles together to close it. It feels familiar, and I realize it is like Anni's stroller.

It takes almost half an hour. Ma Ma lifts her right leg up one step at a time, swings out her left and drags it behind, step by step, consistently stubbing the toe of her new left sneaker. Her right hand grabs heartily for the worn wooden handrail we were not allowed as children to touch because it was crawling with the germs of Old Man Lee, who lived on the top floor. Her left hand holds Tony's, heartily also.

"Tank u, tank u," Ma Ma says. Now she says this almost as often as "Good luck, good luck."

Together they reach her new apartment, the one-bedroom flat on the second floor, number 22, where Ba Ba had lived alone. The landlord had taken advantage of her absence and converted apartment number 12 into full-fledged commercial use and rented it to an insurance company. I have taped a red-and-gold Chinese poster at Ma Ma's new door: an upside-down *fook*, the Chinese character for happiness, to ensure that goodness always returns. "Upside-down" in Chinese sounds like "return."

There is no better fast food than what you find in Chinatown. In the same time it took Ma Ma to struggle up the stairs, I am already returning with two bags of hot lunch whisked from handpicked restaurants known for that specialty. We eat chicken, of course, that animal of the good life that shows up at all celebrations. *Gie*, the Chinese word for "chicken," is similar to the one for "world," *giae*, so chickens are the world, and good chickens mean good world. In more earthly terms, Ma Ma believed that only those who could afford to kill the bearer of eggs feasted on chicken. We grew up eating pork. But today, I buy a whole poached chicken, anemic and white, with a seafoam green dipping sauce of crushed ginger and minced scallion and sea salt. I can't resist the roast pig with the crackling red skin, a favorite of Ma Ma's, and ask for two pounds of the leanest cut. Tomorrow, Ma Ma can have the leftovers steamed with purple Chinese shrimp paste packaged in a jam jar. I must remember to ask Mrs. Chin, her nanny/housekeeper, to buy some. How Kent and I used to fight over the skimpy juice of this dish to mix into our rice. It was our Chinese Hamburger Helper, the stretcher of food dollars. Even now, I prefer the shrimp paste over anchovies, using it in Caesar salad. Besides Tony's roast pork lo mein, I buy noodles crisp-fried brown and topped with assorted sautéed seafood. Ma Ma will love the giant scallops and lobster tail. And the long noodles, a traditional dish we have on birthdays, will wish her a long life. Finally, I stuff the bag with six steamed puffy "cupcakes" for dessert, to bloom our fortune, and a dozen navel oranges for a fruitful future, which Ma Ma will interpret to mean a grandson by her son.

We are fingers deep into the food with barely enough napkins to wipe the grease. This can become a routine, and I make a proposition to Tony. "How about eating roast pork lo mein every week?" He agrees readily, and we arrange for him to visit Ma Ma and help her through her exercise routine every Tuesday and Friday, between 11:00 A.M. and 2:00 P.M. He is a trooper, making his trip on the subway with the portable step, two-pound wraparound ankle weights, and blue three-pound dumbbells. As a bonus for Ma Ma, I arrange for a weekly massage by a Chinese doctor of natural medicine, an herbologist whose hands tell of your ailments and sometimes even cure them.

The glow of the homecoming and the honeymoon with Tony and Dr. Herbologist, however, begins to dim over the first several months. On her own, Ma Ma faces this new life as a new immigrant in another foreign territory. Here life brought her back to Chinatown where she had been stationary for decades because of her carsickness. Even traveling ten miles to our home in the suburbs had been for Ma Ma like a trip to the moon. My carsick mother is now forever bound to a wheelchair.

In the privacy of her home and with only Mrs. Chin, Ma Ma sloppily feeds herself, using only one hand and refusing to wear a bib even though her seamstress friend presented her with several large rectangular bibs, some even in fabric remnants from Ma Ma's old dresses, in bright floral patterns. Greasy lips and fingers on Ma Ma are distasteful, but chocolate cake all over Anni's face and wrists is worthy of a snapshot. What double standards I harbor. While the very qualities that are Ma Ma's nature—her independence and her pride—make her stroke most difficult, they are the strengths that give her the will to live. But oh, Lord, she has to ask someone to feed her, to clothe her, to cleanse her, to push her. To swallow her pride is choking her, and sometimes Ma Ma takes us down with her.

"*Huew gor do.*" Ma Ma points, directing from her wheelchair. Go there. Like a generalette, she shows her new habit of shaking the crooked finger of her good hand to order her wheres and her wants. Everything she wants—big and small—is a demand.

Not so fast, Ma Ma yells.

Pull in your arm, I yell back.

I am amazed to learn that she has asked Tony to come less often, only once a week—too expensive, she said—and Dr. Herbologist to come every other week. And she has stopped taking regular walks in the hallway of her apartment, getting out of her wheelchair only to use the toilet.

I'm tired, she says.

It's good for you, I say.

My mother has become so unbecoming. But so have I, I am forced to learn. I fracture my ankle and, at times wheelchair bound if not up on crutches, I become Ma Ma. *Everything* I want is a demand: a cup of water, my cold coffee nuked, my shoes from over there, my knapsack to be carried. I damn everyone and myself. Then I voluntarily tie my left arm in a sling for a day, forcing myself to use only one hand. I curse trying to unscrew the peanut butter jar, to peel back the aluminum foil on yogurt cups, to gather Mark's playing cards with a rubber band, to squeeze toothpaste onto my toothbrush, to wrap a birthday present. But it isn't so much what I can't do. It is more what I have given up. I am no longer the head engine driving the family forward, but the caboose, feeling like the bumper sticker: "If you're not the lead dog, the view never changes." Even when asked what kind of sandwich or which brand of gum I want, I give up the decision making and say, "Whatever you get for me is fine."

But it isn't fine. I hate losing so much. I imagine myself with unlimited free time on my hands but being too tired to read, unable to knit, too bored with television. My mind is going to putty, the lethargy begetting more lethargy, and my body softens with inactivity. I am trapped in a perpetual state of insomnia, when time seems endless and thoughts roam free, problems and fears loom large and insolvable.

Chapter Thirteen

GONE FISHING

$\mathcal{B}$a Ba's mother had succumbed to the geo man and sent Ba Ba to America for his own good. More than half a century later, I sent him to Staten Island.

On his first day, Ba Ba seemed to take to the camp atmosphere of the nursing home, which was a lone ten-story brick building set in a quiet neighborhood of small detached, wooden houses. The street was too noiseless and too clean.

My defenses were up.

"Hey, Kent, doesn't this place smell like P.S. Twenty-three?" I nudged him with a chuckle. "Why does it always smell like tomato soup?"

"Yeah, and even the walls are the same shade of olive. Must be New York color-challenged green."

We were children joking to mask our uneasiness. We talked too much and said not enough. We sent cryptic warnings to everyone about the goods they were about to receive.

"Well, our father likes to sleep late in the mornings," I said to the head administrator during the admissions interview.

"And he likes it very quiet when he's reading the newspaper," Kent added.

"Oh, really? Well, Mr. Liang"—she turned to Ba Ba—"I think Mr. Choy's the roommate for you."

We followed her down the hall and into the elevator operated by a man who clanged the diamond-gated door shut. Somehow it was like going to the principal's office. We reached Ba Ba's room and were introduced to a sliver of a man who reminded me of peanuts still in the shell. He was slight, and his skin wavy and wrinkly tan. Yes, he seemed just friendly enough not to disturb Ba Ba too much.

But our visits to Ba Ba turned out to be a cross between consciousness raising and gripe airing.

"Hey, your dad won't play cards with me," Mr. Choy said to us. "All he does is play solitaire."

"Humph! Who wants to play with you?" Ba Ba snorted in reply. "So stupid!"

We brought Mr. Choy his own pack of cards, blue for him and red for Ba Ba, on our next visit. Even then, little symmetry existed between them. Mr. Choy lasted a few weeks as Ba Ba's roommate, a victim of Ba Ba's accusations.

"Who ate my crackers?"

"Who took my watch?"

"Who's stealing my money?"

Ba Ba was sure it was Mr. Choy.

Other roommates came and went. Nothing was resolved until Kent brought a second padlock for Ba Ba's cabinet and two for his desk drawer, changing one for the other every weekend to give Ba Ba the illusion of security.

Tomas and I drove weekly from Manhattan to Staten Island in the middle of any afternoon when traffic was lightest and Anni was napping. We always visited Ba Ba with a heavy brown paper bag weighted with a pastrami sandwich on seedless rye for Ba Ba from the deli across the street from our restaurant. The smell of the kosher pickle in the bag led the way. By now, Ba Ba had sifted almost everything from his life, and his hearing seemed to be getting worse. Or maybe he just didn't listen. But he refused to wear his hearing aid. The echoing sound made him dizzy, he said, and disoriented.

Still, Ba Ba asked, "How's Bee?" The exchange always occurred this way. At the doorway. With the pastrami sandwich. Over the question. A sandwich exchange at Checkpoint Charlie. Bee is short for *bee bee*, "tiny precious baby," for Mark. Ba Ba took specially to Bee.

"Bee's great. He's playing the violin. Mozart and Beethoven," Tomas said, as Ba Ba peeked into the stroller at Anni. I could swear he winked.

Then he walked slowly, clopping his slippers and balancing the sandwich to the small table by the window where his newspapers were piled. Carefully, he slid out the mound of sandwich, the pickle wetting the paper and his fingers. Sometimes a thumbnail section of bread would be soaked. He ate only half of a half, reducing the meat and shrinking the three-inch-high sandwich to a mouthable thickness. And, afterward, he locked the other half of his pastrami sandwich in his desk drawer.

•   •   •

Tomas and I were in the middle of the pet-supply aisle buying a plastic habitat for Mark's and Anni's new hamsters, Hammy and Sandwich, when the solution came. Yes, *this* is what Ba Ba needs, not newspapers or locks or sandwiches, but a twenty-five-gallon fish tank just like the one he had always had on Mott Street.

"Look, Ba Ba, look at what we have for you!" Tomas carried in the tank on our next visit, the light cord trailing down, as Anni held a plastic bag of neons and guppies in one hand, a bag of colorful gravel in the other.

"Ohhh, fish," Ba Ba said. "For me?"

"All for you, Ba Ba," I said, "just like we had at home. Remember what you used to say all the time?"

"Don't overfeed them. A little in the morning and a little at night."

We brought water to the tank a pitcherful at a time, and after each pour, Anni wants to put in the fish. Finally, her eyes swoosh in with the fish. We turned on the bubbling pump and watched the rectangular glass for a time as if it were TV. By late afternoon, only the tank lamp lighted the room. We kissed Ba Ba in turn and left midgurgle.

The next week, though, the fish tank was gone.

All Ba Ba said was, "No pets allowed."

Ba Ba lay dying in the hospital and I never went to see him. I never saw his face crumpled like a brown paper bag, his mouth dried and caked with white saliva. I never saw his hands so still and puffy with liquid. I never saw his tan complexion yellowed by illness, his shin bloodied with scratches, his eyes closed and steady, relaxed and somehow focused.

I did not see Ba Ba the day he was admitted nor the day after, which was the day he died.

Kent saw him. Naturally, my big brother took care of everything. He supervised Ba Ba's death. Intellectually. How does a son authorize a doctor to write "DNR" on his father's hospital chart in big red letters? *Do Not Resuscitate.* And emotionally. Smooth his hair. Kiss his forehead. Hold his hand. Allow to die. Send to heaven.

"He didn't seem to feel any pain," Kent said to me in the final phone call in the two-day marathon. I wasn't asking any questions but he gave me the answers anyway. "The night they brought Ba Ba to the hospital, he was feverish. When I saw him lying in the stretcher, he seemed disoriented. He was agitated and incoherent."

At old age, one never dies from death. It is always from complications. The doctors suspected Ba Ba might have the flu, but his condition deteriorated too rapidly. The next day, the hospital did a spinal tap, Kent said, and the diagnosis was bacterial meningitis. By then, Ba Ba was already in a coma and having seizures.

"It would have been very hard to save him," Kent continued, part of him wandering away. The seizure medication given to Ba Ba caused respiratory arrest.

"In the end," Kent finally said, "I thought it happened the best way. Let him go quickly."

A father's daughter is also worth a thousand pieces of gold, as well as hundreds of pastrami sandwiches. But it wasn't enough. The nursing home was just a halfway house for Ba Ba. He spent the time there—in all about one year—waiting. But I always knew he was ready.

Ten years before Ba Ba's actual death, a clarity had come upon him when his past, present, and future lives aligned themselves as if in a solar eclipse, providing rare perspective. Ba Ba asked his longtime bachelor friend, Dr. Frank Lum, our family dentist, to help him leave this world.

"Help me die," Ba Ba said. Later he had replayed the conversation to Kent as though reporting a news event. "Give me rat poison."

"Ho-o-o-o-o!!!" Dr. Lum had laughed, like a Chinese Woody Allen, throwing his head back. "What are you? Crazy?"

"I'm finished," said Ba Ba.

"No, you're crazy!"

This exchange between the two men, friends for more than fifty years, was like a buddy pledge, a hello, a greeting, a parting. Three years later, Dr. Lum was found in his dentist's chair, his own last patient, stone dead. Ba Ba said it was by rat poison.

Ba Ba had tried again to end his life about a year before Ma Ma's stroke. The conversation with Kent had begun casually.

"How are things going, Ba?" Kent had said. It was an ordinary question, one to which the expected answer would be something like, "Fine, thank you. Do you think you can fix this leaky faucet?" These conversations usually took place after Ba Ba's early dinner, that time of day when life takes a lull between the day's end and the evening's start, when Kent stopped by a couple of times a week on his walk home from his office. Most likely Ba Ba would be reading the paper at the funky black-speckled yellow

Formica dining table with a mug of caffeine-free boiled water in his hand.

"Things are just great," Ba Ba began. "You know, I've had a very full life. A happy life. I'm happy that you and Jenny are doing well with your lives. I'm not unhappy, you know.

"I'm getting old, but I'm not too old to know it," Ba Ba continued. "A lot of things are changing. For me. More and more now, I walk into a room and I forget whether I'm going in or coming out. I stand at the doorway and I just don't know which way to go. I read the paper, *The New York Times* or the *Daily News*, every day, but by the time I get to the last page, I forget what I read on the first page. What's the use?"

"Hey, Ba, we all have times we forget. So what?"

"I think it's my time."

"Time for what?" There was a sense of letting go in Ba Ba's voice, a resolve that Kent had heard in patients before. "What are you trying to say, Ba?"

"You're a doctor, Kent." Ba Ba was uncharacteristically direct. "You have your medical license, right? You can prescribe a pill for me, something I can take when I want to go to sleep, sleep without any pain?"

Kent knew what sleep Ba Ba meant. And he was appalled. "This is not ... You can only do that in some countries in Europe. That's called euthanasia. We don't do it here. I swore to be a doctor, to preserve life, not take it away. . . ."

"Ha! Then what good are you?" Ba Ba slammed down his mug like a gavel.

Ba Ba never asked Kent again about sleep. But if Ba Ba's

timing had been different, I imagine he might have found another way, another escape instead of cruising through life like a neon guppy, aloof to the school around him, dazed with the world surrounding him, emotionless to the effects pounding him. He might have found a dream or had some hopes, could have been shining instead of rusty. Our lives as his children could have been glowing instead of dim, and we needn't have been the dinghy between him and Ma Ma in their marriage. As children, Kent and I never questioned why Ba Ba slept till noon on most days. Why most of our regular customers came to see Ma Ma and not Ba Ba. Why Dr. Cheng mostly smiled and Ba Ba mostly didn't. But as adults, we began to try to understand. I read about drugs like Prozac and Zoloft, about a Harvard doctor and anthropologist who himself took one of the anti-depressant drugs and who referred to "a formerly suicidal elderly man [who] takes real pleasure in every day." I read this line, again and again, and superimposed Ba Ba over this faceless John Doe.

Before Tomas and I were married, a good friend gave me an engagement present: an hour-long session with a soothsayer, a young woman from Africa, oddly aged, in her Upper West Side apartment. My friend had heard of her power to "see" at an East Side restaurant where diners can have a tarot card reading with their dinner and coffee.

As Edna DuMont sat opposite me, on the other side of a scuffed wooden coffee table brown like her skin, I said very little, not to be outsmarted by giving away clues. I even cleverly brought my tape recorder, but Mrs. DuMont refused to let me use it, saying it would interfere with her sight. She did make certain I was correct about her name.

"Capital D, capital M," she said, in a voice melodic and

earthy, a voice deserving of a recorder. She referred to herself in the third person, as though she were not present, saying things like "Mrs. DuMont allows you to take notes" and "You may ask Mrs. DuMont three questions."

The hour seemed like three minutes, and I walked out of apartment 15B smelling the cooking stew in the hallway and remembering only three things she said:

1) Yes, I should marry him. (I did.)
2) He has big hands and was an open book. You can trust him. (I do.)
3) A small dog scampered over her feet. (What?!)

I took great comfort in what Mrs. DuMont told me. It was all in rebellion of Ma Ma, who could not accept the man I would marry because he was not a Cantonese Chin or Lee, not even a Hwang from northern China, but a foreign ghost from as outlandish a place as *Eastern* Europe. How can you trust someone from a country you don't know? And the dog! A pet dog was never a consideration in our family for we were like many Chinese who generalized dogs as scrawny, dirty animals, strays in search of food in garbage cans tucked in alleys. More likely pets for us were colorful birds in bamboo cages, crickets with pretty voices, or fish with unbothersome beauty.

But after Mark was born, Tomas and I were on our usual afterdinner walk through the commercial bustle of Eighth Street in Greenwich Village. I could close my eyes and name the shops one after the other, first the sparse shoe store, then the leather handbag shop, then the hi-fi "designer" up a few steps. Tonight, we stopped for a long look in the window of the American Kennel Club, and even went in. We walked out with a dog, a three-month-old short-haired red dachshund, just like the one Tomas had had as a boy on his grandmother's European valley farm. We named him Max.

After Ba Ba died, there was something about Max's look, his furled brow, his aimless demeanor, that became somehow very familiar to me. Max often stood in the middle of nowhere, looking into the air, staring straight ahead in the direction where his nose happened to be pointed. He did nothing. He said nothing. It came to me that this, this simple, honest animal, was Ba Ba. This was Ba Ba when he courted Ma Ma in Hong Kong, when he watched the fire in our apartment, when he visited Ma Ma in the hospital, when he himself lay dying in the same hospital.

I thought of the words on the plaque above the ashes of a famous Indian guru: "Never Born. Never Died. Only Visited This Planet Earth." Having felt out of sorts on earth, Ba Ba was ready, ready for something he could not identify. I thought of the guru's words and knew myself to be in Ba Ba's company every day.

He hasn't died. He has just gone fishing.

Chapter Fourteen

MMM HO QUA SUM,

DON'T HANG YOUR HEART

ON ANY WORRY

$\mathcal{M}$y parents were kites flying one high above the other, never in synchronization, circling each other with looks of distance and distrust, menacing each other with threats of severing the other's string. Their marriage had been a flying contest. And for a while Ba Ba seemed to be the winner, his string having cut Ma Ma's, striking her down with her stroke. But without her loft, he would soon follow and spiral down behind her.

And then, what would become of Ma Ma?

"Don't talk about him anymore," Ma Ma said when Kent and I, each holding one of her hands, told her of Ba Ba's illness and death. She listened, cocking her head to her right, and I tried to discern some emotion, any emotion, in her hand or in her eyes.

"But do you forgive him?" I needed to know.

Kent would later challenge me. "Forgive him for what?"

"For not supporting her."

"She didn't need it from him. She was too strong."

"Even if she was, she still wanted him to be there. She was so alone."

Kent would come to a different perspective of Ba Ba, no longer caring that Ba Ba had lashed at him for not getting an A this semester in social studies like last semester, for reading *A Catcher in the Rye* with curse words, for getting mail from SDS, Students for a Democratic Society, and from Cuba. Was it a girl? Was it pornography? Was he a Communist? Ma Ma was always escalating the arguments, Kent said; she didn't know how to treat Ba Ba. She was powerless under him, I said, she just wanted him to appreciate her. She was convinced Ba Ba did not love her. But both Kent and I would come to agree that Ba Ba just didn't know how. It was the best he could do.

But does Ma Ma forgive him?

"No. I hate him," she said. "I hate him, for everything he's done to me. Don't talk about him. I want to forget him."

I realized it was the best she could do. He no longer existed for her.

Ba Ba had been like a pebble in her shoe she could not shake. Now that pebble was gone.

Tomas leaned low to kiss Ma Ma on both cheeks, first on the right, then on the left. Even with so many of the muscles in her body incapacitated by her stroke, Ma Ma managed to remember to tilt her head left, then right in anticipation of his two kisses. Even her hair swung left and right. Sometimes Tomas and Ma Ma would even meet in the middle when both leaned in the same direction, bumping noses. It was Tomas's European way, his way among so many that were ever so appealing. Ma Ma lifted her right arm toward him from the armrest of her wheelchair in slow motion, like the replay of a tennis serve without the racquet. She reached with her small hand wrapped in crinkly tan skin for Tomas's smooth pink palm, tucking her fingers into his large ones.

"Hello, Ma Ma. I'm happy to see you," he said between kisses. They shared the breath between them, an intimacy unlikely a few years ago. I could feel Tomas's sense of rush, standing so tall next to my seated Ma Ma, not only his innate impatience and unwillingness to wait for anything, but also the actual dash he had already made that morning to open the restaurant and to set up the manager with the day's cash register tills, the meat and bread orders to be called in, the appointment confirmed with the liquor salesman. In between, Tomas had stopped at the bank to deposit last night's money. He probably parked his car illegally in front of the fire hydrant at the entrance of Ma Ma's apartment building, and he probably double stepped up the flight of stairs. I can bet on it.

"Hello, Tomas, you came so early today," Ma Ma said, no longer words squeezed out between tilted lips but clear, loving sounds. She even seemed to pull his hand to bring him closer to her.

"*Nay gum yut ho ma*, Ma Ma? How do you feel today, Ma Ma?" Tomas asked. He caught on early with Chinese baby talk, then with the obvious Chinese questions, even broadening his vocabulary to include, "Ma Ma, *nay meen sic ho ho*. Your skin, your coloring, looks very good. *Nay yeow sic.* Get your rest. *Mmm ho qua sum.* Don't hang your heart on any worry." These were the only times Ma Ma laughed, chuckles that spurted with great effort, that sometimes led to coughs of merriment. Tomas's words were like offkey music.

Tomas stayed bent over her wheelchair, holding her hand in the type of hold you use for arm wrestling. Ma Ma was coming of age in her own way. Her left hand, limp with the plain silver wedding band she has never taken off, lay on her abdomen.

"You are the *best* husband, Tomas," Ma Ma said right into his ear. "I love you, love you very much. You take good care of Jenny and the children." She was gushy and blushing.

"Tomas, you can tell a man by his hands," Ma Ma continued, still holding his hand, turning it palm side up. "Look at your hands, Tomas, they're soft. I know you use your brains. You are not a laborer, a farmer or a peasant, but you are a learned man, educated, an intellectual. My father was like that. His fingers were so long and slender, the skin so fine and pale.

"And your hands, Tomas," she continued, lining up his fingers, "here's a man of good fortune, not only fortune for money and material wealth, but also for goodness that comes from the heart. I can tell your heart is lined with goodness. Look, there are no gaps between your fingers so your good fortune will never seep away. That's why many Chinese men wear gold bands, you know? To stop the gaps and keep their money and luck from slipping away."

Ma Ma let go, raising her right hand to touch Tomas's face. Feel your round, thick earlobes, Ma Ma said, like the ones you see on statues of Buddha. And your chin, look for a strong chin that scoops up, a sign that a man is worth the wealth he makes and will not lose it to someone who outsmarts him or to gambling. Like yours. She smoothed her hand over Tomas's face, running from his plump earlobes to his firm massive chin.

Watch out for types like Henry Leung, she warned. Here's a man with a hooked nose who would surely bring an early death to his wife, just as a woman like Mary Wu with a high forehead would bring on an early death to her husband. A man like George Lee who walked on his toes could not be trusted, nor could you count on a man like Joe Gee whose jaws you can see from behind his head. Imagine that, you could see part of his face from the back! Be careful of men who are always picking their teeth with a toothpick. They're the laziest of all. And men who shake their legs, all that nervous energy. Stay away from them. All they have is sex on their mind.

I never looked at Tomas piecemeal like that, dissecting him like a first-year medical student. How do you describe a feeling in the heart to a Chinese mother? She only understood what the eye could see. She would love Tomas for not smoking, for not drinking, for not gambling. She would love Tomas for not having a mistress, for not going to prostitutes, for not having a concubine. She would love Tomas for emptying his pockets of everything every day, all of his money, the business cards he collected, the phone numbers he needed to call. Emptied them for me. Ma Ma would love him that he has no secrets. She would love him that all he owns are possessions for his wife and children, and all he does, he does for us. And now she was finally saying it. To him. For me.

"Tomas, I love you the most," she repeated.

"Ma Ma, after Jenny and the kids, I love *you* the most." Tomas laughed.

Chapter Fifteen

VACATION A MONTH

$\mathcal{K}$ent married Melinda in a civil ceremony on New Year's Eve, to which no one was invited except the cleaning lady in the hall who signed as a witness. By then, Melinda had joined Kent's office staff as the billing and financial manager, and she flowed an elaborate wedding on a computer spreadsheet to show Kent how a no-frills wedding made incredible sense. Melinda calculated what they would save, divided it by twelve, and booked a "vacation a month" for the next year—going to places like Santa Fe and Singapore, Vienna and Vietnam, Cancun and Curaçao. And Melinda saw to the completion of the kitchen, which is centered with a forest-green granite island and cabinets of bubinga wood, and the rest of the loft, which is as un-Oriental as you can get, no artistic scrolls of mountain scenery on the walls, no carved wood chairs with shiny silk cushions, no pagoda lamps with ivory shades.

Kent chose the occasion of his thirty-ninth birthday soon thereafter to tell Ma Ma about his marriage.

Ma Ma reached out her right hand as though she were pointing her forefinger toward Melinda's shoes, and Melinda bent down to kiss her. "Melinda, welcome to our family," Ma Ma said. "I hope I am as lucky as Great-Auntie Moy. She handpicked her daughter-in-law, and today, at age eighty, she has two grandsons and not one worry. Her son and daughter-in-law take care of everything."

"Thank you, Mrs. Liang," Melinda said. "I hope I won't disappoint you."

Ma Ma turned to me, still holding Melinda's hand. "Jenny, pass me that box," Ma Ma directed. "Yes, the box with the small red tiles." She was pointing her scraggly finger at a wooden box just the size to hold two decks of cards, a box she had crafted at Randal. She struggled to pull off the lid, unable to grasp the box's bottom with her left hand, and I helped her by holding the bottom while she yanked. Inside the box was a small stack of *hoong bows*, red envelopes. This I wanted to see, how much money would Ma Ma give to a new daughter-in-law. How much was *she* worth? But Ma Ma bypassed the money and pulled out a small wad of tissue bound with a thin red rubber band.

"Melinda, here, this is for you." Ma Ma plunked the tissue ball into her hand. As Melinda unwound the linty tissue, the glint emerging from Melinda's palm hurt my eyes. It was Ma Ma's solitaire emerald-cut diamond engagement ring, the one gift she received from Ba Ba that she cherished, for it represented her transformation from an Eng to a Liang, a symbol of the continuation of the family name.

"I have been saving this," Ma Ma was saying, "saving this for Kent's wife, for you, my daughter-in-law."

I looked urgently at Kent. "You have to tell her," I murmured. He still hadn't told her that there would be no children.

"What do you think I am—stupid?" he murmured back. "I'll tell her someday."

"You can't let her think—"

"Shut up, Jenny. Can't you just stay out of it?"

Ma Ma cocked her head. "What are you two saying?" she demanded.

How can I let Kent get away with it? "You're not going to be like Great-Auntie Moy," I said.

"What do you mean?" Ma Ma was unusually quick.

"Nothing," Kent was even quicker. "Jenny means nothing."

Melinda intruded. "Thank you very much for the ring, Mrs. Liang," she said. "I will treasure this."

"You can call me Ma Ma."

Kent and I did not talk to each other for several months after that. Melinda, now my sister-in-law, often met me for lunch in Chinatown at a steamy restaurant where they boiled the wonton and noodles right there in the dining room. This afternoon, with filthy snow piled on the sidewalk garbage and extra steam in the restaurant from the radiators and the cooking pots fogging Melinda's eyeglasses, we scrunched ourselves into sharing a table with an elderly man and his granddaughter.

"How do you like working for Kent?" I asked, slurping the blendered mango drink with tapioca almost too thick to suck through a straw. Melinda had done the ordering, and she certainly knew her way around food.

"It's getting better as I'm learning what he likes," Melinda said.

"Well, you don't always have to do what *he* wants. You know, my father used to rewrite the price tags for the shop because he didn't like my mother's handwriting. Can you imagine that?"

"Nothing's wrong with that," Melinda said, business-like and professional, taking a long draw on her mango drink, "if it makes the price tags more legible."

I frowned. "Any new riddles from Ma Ma recently?" I asked. I plopped a knot of cellophane rice noodles tied into a bow, called "dragon whiskers," into my mouth. It was delicious, especially the feel of the curl on my tongue. "You were really clever how you handled them."

Melinda laughed. "Ma Ma's the clever one. Just the other day, she asked me whether I knew the trick in con-ceiving a baby boy. I played dumb. I said I would be hon-ored to have her tell me her trick."

"That's not dumb. That's smart."

"Ma Ma said, 'I don't tell everyone this technique, only those who are dearest to me. A male grandchild by you and Kent would be very dear indeed.'

"Ma Ma leaned forward and whispered to me. 'Right after the man deposits his male potion in the woman, you have to turn and lie on your right side. Stay on your side. Don't turn until the morning. *Yut ding.* Guaranteed. You'll have a son. It worked for me. Look at Kent. Remember, it's the right side.'"

"Notice how it went from a 'woman' to 'you' specifically," I said. "What did you say?"

"Oh, I asked her how a baby girl was made. And she said, 'Of course, you lie on your left side, but you don't need to know that now. Remember, it's your *right* side.'"

Right side. Left side. Even male potion. Ma Ma's stroke had given her a new boldness and new urgency. She had always been in such a hurry in life, the way she wrote, the way she talked, the way she chopped meat with the cleaver. And now, hindered not at all, she must hasten even more to outrun the future.

Our conversation was slowing down our attack on the tapioca and noodles. We concentrated on slurping our lunch, each waiting for the other to draw first.

"Jenny, you probably know I have endometriosis. . . ."

"Yes . . ."

"Kent told you?"

"Yes, he did. But I don't really know what it means."

"It means it's very difficult for me to have children—maybe never."

With the snow outside and the steam inside, I was once again astounded by Melinda's sangfroid. As we finished lunch, she took off her glasses and placed them on the table. I saw the resolution in her eyes. And for the first time I noticed she wasn't wearing Ma Ma's diamond ring.

For her part, Ma Ma was just as determined. She asked the same of everyone, all the time, tirelessly.

"When will Melinda grant me a grandson?" she would ask of Kent.

"Hello, Melinda, when?" Ma Ma would say and search at her belly.

"When will Kent grant me a grandson?" Ma Ma would ask of me.

For a year, I indulged her. "Soon. Someday. Give her time." I felt I had to protect Melinda, but I resented it all the same.

Right before Kent's first wedding anniversary at Christmastime, I had just picked up Vicki, home from college, at the airport and went to Ma Ma's to set up her small Christmas tree. She still had the three-foot tree we had as children with electric candle ornaments that were tubes of bubbling colored water. Kent stopped by after office hours to prepare Ma Ma's weekly supply of insulin needles, kept on the top shelf of her refrigerator, the upright sticks of injections in the plastic cup stocked next to the container of skim milk. Vicki and Mark still refuse to get milk from Grand Ma Ma's refrigerator.

"Ask him yourself, Ma Ma," I said. "Kent's here." I plugged in the tree and waited for the lights to warm up.

"Hi," Kent said. "Ask what?"

"When are you and Melinda giving me a grandson?" I have never seen Ma Ma so blunt. "Give me a baby boy to cherish."

"Damn it!" Kent bubbled over like the Christmas lights. "Why do you keep asking this of me? You've got your own ass to worry about. Look at yourself. You can't take care of yourself. How can you take care of another grandchild?"

Kent flashed a look at me. Was he accusing me of betrayal or pleading for help? Mrs. Chin retreated to the kitchen. In an instant, Kent's explosion was like Ba Ba's. But I couldn't really blame him. Ma Ma *was* becoming our child. I must have looked like an understanding mother, for Kent softened immediately.

"Ma Ma, listen to me, listen to what I say," he began, holding her hand. Kent always had good bedside manners. "Ma Ma, give up on this grandson idea. Melinda and I will probably never have children."

"What? What did you say? What do you mean?"

"Melinda. Melinda cannot have a baby," Kent said. "She cannot. She has a medical condition that affects her fertility."

"Melinda? Melinda cannot have children? Melinda cannot have children," Ma Ma repeated. "How can this be? But you are a doctor!"

"She's always had a lot of pain every month, Ma Ma, you know, when a woman has her menstruation," I said. "She's been to many specialists. . . ."

"I have known a long time, Ma Ma, and we have tried to find help," Kent said, "but now it's not important to us anymore. We are *very* happy the way it is."

"Melinda, Melinda cannot have children. . . ." Ma Ma repeated.

"What are we going to do? What am I going to do?" Ma Ma went on, caught in her own groove. "How can this be? After all I have sacrificed for you?"

Chapter Sixteen

JICK FOOK,

ACCRUED HAPPINESS

$\mathcal{S}$omewhere in the middle of my childhood, Ba Ba had turned his profession as a photographer into a hobby. Because I would stand still, I was more often than my brother the object on the other side of his lens. If Ba Ba was not at Columbus Park congregating beside a park bench with a newspaper rolled under his arm and discussing the news with other men dressed in tweed overcoats, he was shooting pictures of me looking down into his Rolleiflex camera that he anchored against his bellybutton and that presented him with full-sized negatives. Perfectionist that he was, Ba Ba used a cable release because pushing a button shutter would shake the camera and affect the focus. Favoring the afternoon light and the smooth white stone surface of the city municipal buildings, Ba Ba had taken to photographing us in earnest, always squatting low to shoot up, saying it made the subject seem taller and slimmer and the face more angular.

"See, these pictures are different from passport photos," he would say, setting up the shot. "With those, you have to show the person's ears. The government can always tell your true identity by them because you cannot fake who you are if they can see your ears."

I still have my boxes of photos, in black-and-white and in color, my boxes of Ba Ba's affection. See this one with Kent and me in pajamas sitting on the couch with inverted boat hats on our heads? We had just taken Ba Ba's newspapers and made the hats, and he snapped a photo before he got mad at us. See this one with me in curly locks and a dolly? It was the Christmas before I turned seven and it was my first perm. My eyes are watering from the stench. See this one of me looking at the mobile at the Guggenheim Museum? I was twelve and showing Yee Ma the sights of New York City when she first arrived in the United States. Look closely at my finger and you'll see my first gold band from Hong Kong.

Somewhere in the middle of my adulthood, I became the family photographer. See this one of Vicki at age nine on Dumbo at Disneyworld? That's when Tomas bought her a Mickey Mouse watch, thereafter named the Shitty Watch, because it fell into the toilet. And this one of Mark learning to walk on the beach in Barbados? Everyone thought he was the friendliest baby, waving all the time from Vicki's arms, when he was actually imitating the motion of the ceiling fans. And here's one of Anni riding a camel in Morocco. She vomited right afterward because it made her carsick. The memories that my children have of the places they have visited are not from their memory but from my photos.

1991: This is a photo of all of us on my fortieth birthday. Well, it was a time for taking inventory of my life. Yes, I would always be a perfectionist, but perhaps my day would not be ruined if the alarm clock was set at 6:46 A.M. and not 6:45, if the dishwasher wasn't loaded to my specifications, if the bread's cellophane bag wasn't expertly tied by me.

Auntie Win-Da had begun slowing down, her back caving in a little, her bones still rigid but frail. Her footsteps now poked the pavement, her dresses now cowl necked and even puffy at the sleeves, an attempt to give her frame more fullness. When she retired full-time, Kent asked me to take over as his office manager, and I stepped into Auntie Win-Da's Post-it notes and legible appointment books as seamlessly as Ba Ba would have.

Of course the job constantly spilled over into managing Ma Ma as well. I often brought a boxed Chinatown lunch to share with her and discovered that she liked sharing my can of ginger ale more.

"Ohhhh, it's so fizzy." Ma Ma sipped, winking and grimacing, the same sourpuss face as Tomas's when he drank grapefruit juice with tortilla chips.

"But I *like* it. So spicy, the bubbles and the ginger." Ma Ma sipped to the slurp at the end of the can, tilting it and shaking it to find every drop. "I *like* it, but I don't. Ohhhh, what can you do?"

I wrote a note for Mrs. Chin—"diet ginger ale"—to

add to her shopping list. Kent promptly rewrote it—
"DIET GINGER ALE." "She won't be able to match the
lowercase letters to the ones on the can," he said.

I thought of Ba Ba rewriting Ma Ma's price tags.

Yes, what *can* you do?

1992: This photo of Ma Ma on one of her infrequent
visits to us when Anni had just turned five is a rare one of
her taken outdoors. It was late afternoon, the time and the
season wrapping the park near our home in orange summer sunlight. Anni was basking in that wondrous time
when a true sense of separateness occurs in children, running with freedom and independence like never before
from slide to swing to seesaw and back again. Ma Ma
watched with an acceptance like never before from her
wheelchair, the glow in her eyes not from the setting sun. It
was as though the weight of her own life had lifted and her
existence transcended like a soul to the body of her family.
That moment, I am somehow very sure, Ma Ma came to
terms with her own limitations, finally able to vicariously,
fully enjoy. She had passed on her torch of mobility. She
is—I am—free again.

1993: This is a photo of all of us on Anni's sixth
birthday.

Notice how Ma Ma's hair is cut blunt across the back,
just like in her wedding picture.

For a long time I had worn my hair short, compact at
the crown, very short bangs high across my forehead, and a
W carved at the nape of my neck. It was the creation of my

friend Hito on class night, a three-hour cut that promoted him from floor assistant to full stylist. But since Ma Ma's stroke, my hair had grown out along with Ma Ma's.

On impulse, I asked Hito to make a house call. But first, I took him out to a Chinatown lunch—a change from the sushi bars he usually went to, and I gave him a culinary tour. Isn't this Chinese salted fish similar to your Japanese snacks? Isn't this pickled cabbage in soup like what you eat in salad? Isn't this broad *chow fun* noodle like your thick *udon* noodle? We were still talking about food with ice cream cones in hand when we climbed the stairs to Ma Ma's.

Was it Hito's accent? Was it the way he put forward his hand? But Ma Ma knew immediately.

"Jenny, this boy is Japanese," Ma Ma said to me in Chinese. Her face darted from me to Hito and back to me. "Am I right?"

"How do you know he's Japanese?" I said.

"I can tell."

In a moment all the stories she had told me while I was doing my homework at her knees were embodied in Hito. He was no longer simply a hip pal. He was probably, most likely, the grandson of a Japanese soldier who once aimed a rifle at Ma Ma in China and missed, who made my Grand Ma Ma sleep for years during World War II in a Chinese village with the family money and jewels sewn into the hem of her nightgown, who made her lie about how much food and rice she had so it wouldn't be stolen. All of the talk between Hito and me about cabbage and noodles meant nothing beside Ma Ma's talk about guns and rice.

"So, you don't want Hito to cut your hair?" I asked.

Ma Ma's square jaw relaxed. "He's a person just like we are, isn't he?" She dipped her chin into her chest to allow Hito to start cutting.

Hito combed and cut, combed and cut, and I watched Ma Ma's hair and a lot else fall to the floor in sync with the clicking scissors.

Hito did my hair next.

And that was how I came to have hair like Ma Ma's.

1994: See this photo of Ma Ma on her seventy-sixth birthday? I started a second birthday book for Ma Ma, backtracking it over the past six years, highlighting it with portraits and family snapshots on all birthdays, and today, this was one of her gifts. This year, I again replaced her toilet seat, this time in "new and lighter" but more durable plastic but the same eight inches high. Did you know that toilet seats keep getting reinvented with new materials and designs, like tennis rackets and skis? Two weeks after I delivered a new shower seat to her, she mentioned to me only in passing how the old one was better. Was it softer? I asked. No, she said. The old one had a U-shaped cushion, and it was so much easier for washing down there!

Ma Ma did not just hang on. She was thriving. She even seemed healthier than before her stroke and now was downright robust. Her heart was strong and she was eating well. Her job now was to be the keeper of birthdays.

"Ma Ma, whose birthday is coming up next?" I asked.

"Oh, it's June, June seventeen. It's Anni's."

"And when is Vicki's?" I continued the game.

"Vicki's? Vicki's is, I think, in October … October twelve. October twelve."

"You remember, Ma Ma!"

"Yes, and Mark's too. Mark's is February. That's right. After the new year. February four. Right?"

1995: In this photo, Mark is holding up all ten fingers for his tenth birthday. "I'm double digits now!" Mark exclaimed throughout the day. During his birthday dinner at Grand Ma Ma's, Mark insisted on lighting his own candles again and again and blowing them out. He has always liked matches, more precisely fire, and we let him strike the matches to his heart's content for his birthday cake, which became only half-edible because of the plentiful wax.

Grand Ma Ma, who would not have indulged in this dangerous behavior before, was delighted. Their eyes glowed together.

"He is so full of life," she said. "He is so bright, not only intelligent but also bright in spirit. Do you know?"

Ma Ma was quiet as Mark opened his presents, this computer game and that. Not that I was rushing him, but I gave Mark a razor and aerosol cream for his birthday. I marveled at Mark the way I used to watch Ba Ba shave in the bathroom mirror. It was a ritual from my childhood: the spiral, ballish handle on the shaving brush; the round wooden bowl of Yardley shaving soap; the razor neither double-edged nor disposable. Every day, without fail, Ba Ba slapped his cheeks with a few dabs of lukewarm water, grasped the wooden brush and swirled it round the bowl clockwise three times. Eyeing himself seriously in the mirror, he applied the softly bubbled soap carefully to all the crevices of his face. Ballooning his cheeks to pull his skin taut, Ba Ba raised the razor to below his eye and started out and down, carefully and caressingly. Time stopped when he was shaving; he never rushed. The bathroom door was always open, and I was always there, whether with my chin barely above the sink or standing with my shoulder against the door.

Ma Ma had been too quiet watching, mostly Mark now playing with the swelling creaminess of the shaving foam, giving the menthol a whiff.

"Kent," she finally said. "My diamond engagement ring. I gave it to you, for Melinda, a few years ago . . . when you got married.

"I would like to have the ring back. I want to give it to Mark for his birthday. He is a young man now and someday he will get married and maybe, maybe he will have children. Watch, I will live to see that!"

Mark roared at idea of getting married and having children and continued playing with his new toys, particularly the tumbling remote control car, whirring it in and around Ma Ma's wheelchair.

1996: Here is a photo of Ma Ma's seventy-eighth birthday. She is wearing a new red shawl, one of her favorite accessories, preferring it to hooded sweatshirts. On her lap is the red tartan plaid blanket we had cut in half to share between her and Anni.

All her life, Ma Ma had worried about not having a good husband, not having enough money, not living a long life. She is proving herself wrong.

"Are you happy, Ma Ma?" I asked.

"Yes, my *cheen gum*, my thousand pieces of gold," she said. "How can I not be happy? What have I to worry about?"

I smiled.

She continued. "I don't worry about money. There is no war, no famine. I don't have to run from soldiers. I'm not even a refugee from a bad marriage. I don't have to flee from a bad husband!"

"Ma Ma, what would make you happier?" I asked.

I wished I hadn't. Ma Ma has not been idle in her wheelchair. "To be happier? When I die, I want you to know what I want . . . what would make me happy."

But who asked her about death? "You're not going to die! *Dai gut lai see.* Don't talk like that. And don't think like that."

She continued anyway. "Not until you're almost dead do you know what you need to live."

Somewhere I had heard this before.

"When I die, I want to be cremated. Nothing fancy, okay?" she said, satisfaction in her voice. "Throw me to the wind. Then, that's that! No urns of ashes for you to carry around."

This was her birthday wish.

1996: Oh yes. This is the photo of Mark and Anni hamming it up with their pig-snout faces on Stephans-platz in Vienna. We made this one into Christmas cards that year. For several years, Tomas had been developing business ventures in Eastern Europe after the fall of the Iron Curtain, and finally we decided to move there. But how could we leave Ma Ma? I did not even know how to say Czechoslovakia in Chinese when I told Ma Ma of our plans.

"Follow your husband," she said. "If he walks fast, walk fast with him. If he walks slowly, walk slowly."

How does Ma Ma know? That wheelchair was good for something after all.

1997: Here we are in an Airbus 300 flying back from Europe for Ma Ma's seventy-ninth birthday. Mark and Anni helped Grand Ma Ma blow out all of the candles on her birthday cake, Mark delighted to strike two entire boxes of matches. Vicki, in her second year of medical school, divvied up Ma Ma's pills into the cubicled pill case and prepared her insulin needles. We brought Ma Ma a dozen oranges, and I pulled off the skin with my fingers and put the wedges, one by one, in her mouth. Then Anni fed her, bite for bite, a jumbo rice cake, alternating sips of tea. We watched as Ma Ma put on her sneakers side by side with Anni, truly appreciating the ironic symmetry as she dealt with Velcro tabs while her granddaughter raced with her laces. Even though Ma Ma has little occasion to write, she leaned earnestly over Anni's shoulder when she penned her homework in script, which in its round and scraggly way resembled Ma Ma's handwriting.

I wore the jade cuff bracelet, chunky and green like a Granny Smith apple, that Ma Ma had saved for me in the safe deposit box, enjoying the pale green cool against my wrist. It was the only piece of jewelry I wore. I've given up on glamour although I still hang on to my twenty-plus white cotton shirts of all designs and twenty-plus pairs of black Italian shoes. Still, this year, Mark's birthday present to me was The Most Balanced Person Award, a clay statue he had sculpted of an Atlas painted red with blue shorts, arms outstretched overhead, holding what looks like a giant surfboard. It started out as "The Strongest Person," Mark explained, but the round weight above the surfboard broke off, and he renamed it. Anyway, he said, being balanced is more important than being strong.

I watched Ma Ma's face shine before her candlelit cake. She was carefree as a child, living only for the sake of living. She puts her best efforts into eating well and sleeping well—and into having a good bowel movement. Ma Ma always said the last ten years of your life are the most telling, the true measure of your life as a whole. Sometimes I think her stroke may have actually prolonged her life.

We crowded around her to take family photos with my new camera. I was fussing with the new buttons and gadgets, trying to get a series of Ma Ma sitting in her wheelchair with her three grandchildren behind her. The kids pushed each other, jostling to put their head closest to Grand Ma Ma's, and gave each other rabbit ears while doing so. Mark made a funny face, and Anni tried to outdo him. Vicki was trying to tickle them to at least break the crunched faces into smiles. They reached down and rubbed Grand Ma Ma's large belly for good luck, moving their hands in unison on her tummy, feeling her softness through three layers of clothes, saying too loudly into her ears, "We love you more, Grand Ma Ma." I could feel the goosebumps on her skin. She laughed, her belly shaking, and said, "I love *you* more."

Then Anni broke the rhythm, and said, "You are Q," to Grand Ma Ma, who sang back, "*You* are Q!" This was their theme song ever since they discovered Grand Ma Ma always forgot to pronounce the *t* in cute. "*No, nay Q dee!* No, you are cuter!" Each tried to have the final word.

"Ma Ma, you really have *jick fook*," I said, clicking the camera. You've accumulated such happiness, I told her. Her smile was totally unabashed.

"Yes, yes, I really, really have *jick fook*," Ma Ma repeated. You know, it's as though she has this white picket fence, and each and every slat is perfectly white and upright except one. She no longer focuses on the crooked slat, and neither do we.

By the way, this photo is one of the best pictures we have of Ma Ma.